ROMANCE RESET

MAKE ME A MATCH SERIES

KAY LYONS

KINDRED SPIRITS PUBLISHING

Copyright

ROMANCE RESET Copyright © 2020 by Kay Lyons

Cover art © 2020 @ alessandroguerr

Cover art design © 2020 Kindred Spirits Publishing

ROMANCE RESET

"You did wha— *Seriously?*" Amelia Parker asked, blown away by the news her best friend had just dropped like a bomb. "You hired a matchmaker? For *me*?"

"Yes, for you," Izzy said. "Meli, you Googled directions to sperm banks and checked out their Yelp reviews."

"I was researching. That's no reason to go crazy a- and hire a *matchmaker*." It wasn't that she was anti-matchmaker but what the process meant. She'd made a firm decision about using a sperm bank to get the family she wanted. Trying her hand at dating—again—messed with that plan. And with her biological clock ticking… Time wasn't on her side.

"Yeah, hiring a matchmaker is the crazy in that scenario. If you're willing to go that route just because the big four-oh looms in the distance—"

"Not that distant."

"*Then* there is no reason not to try my idea first," Izzy said as though Amelia hadn't interrupted her.

"Meli, you've given up on love and romance and I can't stand it."

The noise of the restaurant faded into the background as Amelia stared into the concerned expression of her friend. The fat-paddle fans overhead kept the air flowing, but nothing could cool the heat flooding Amelia's body due to stress.

"Says the woman who is as single as I am." Izzy was an artist Amelia had met four years ago after consigning a special piece for a particular movie set. They'd hit it off and become fast friends. But shouldn't a friend know not to mess with another friend's plans?

"That may be so but I'm not trying to be a baby mama. You seriously don't want to raise a kid alone, do you?"

"Who says if I'm with someone he'll stick around? Do you know how many single parents are in the world? I know it'll be difficult, but why not save myself the heartache of meeting someone only to have them walk out later?"

"Wow. Cynical much?"

Amelia glared at Izzy. "Wait until you're my age. I've pretty much seen it all." Izzy was ten years younger than Amelia and obviously wasn't worried about children any time soon. Izzy had issues with her two biological sisters, and not for the first time did Amelia wonder if Izzy's stubbornness and persistence had something to do with the difficulties within her immediate family.

"You're doing this," Izzy said. "You're meeting her. I won't hear another word about it."

Izzy tilted her head as she stared at Amelia and wore what Amelia always thought of as Izzy's *booya* expression. Izzy widened her very expressive eyes and set her jaw, lips pursed in a determined line. "So is she setting you up, too?" Time to change tactics. Obviously getting out of the mess wasn't an option, so maybe she should drag Izzy along for the ride?

"No. At least not yet, anyway. Look, you mentioned meeting Marsali Jones on the set of the movie set you're designing, *and* that she's a friend of Oliver Beck's. He's a freaking Hollywood actor and friends with this woman. She's obviously got something, and if *anyone* can help you find the perfect man, I think she can. You know I'm right."

"Izzy—"

"You said how well you and Marsali hit it off, so I decided to take it a step further and contact her for you. She loves the idea, by the way, and thinks the world of you."

"*You told her?*"

"Only that you're ready to settle down with a family. Anyway, she sang your praises and said she knows she can find you a wonderful match."

Amelia groaned and buried her face in her hands. "I'm going to strangle you. Poison you. Push you off a boat into the Intercoastal."

"Yeah, yeah. Come on, Meli, you're embarrassed about being set up by a professional matchmaker, but you're not embarrassed about knowing which sperm banks have a better selection of swimmers?"

That comment was delivered right as their waitress stopped by their table to deliver their drinks, and Amelia nearly dove under the wooden surface. She wasn't shy by nature but certain things needed to remain private. Like their talk of sperm banks and her plan to use one in order to become a mom. "She's joking," Amelia said to the teenager.

"Am not," Izzy countered in a low, singsong voice once the waitress left their drinks and was out of earshot.

"Why do you think me having a baby is a problem?" Amelia asked, continuing the argument with her so-called friend.

"It's the way you're going about it that I have a problem with. That and the fact you think you can pick a kid from a catalogue of characteristics when picking men that way hasn't worked out for you."

"Owwwch." Didn't Izzy get it? She was tired. Tired of searching, tired of looking for the right man only to be disappointed. She'd spent the last twenty-three *years* dating. Maybe not seriously at first, but later she'd tried and wanted more but never found it. And the sad fact was that men her age were now searching for younger women because *they* were finally ready to settle down and have families, and her age factored into a rela-tionship.

"Today you're hearing truth," Izzy argued. "All truth and nothing but. I'm tired of sugarcoating my thoughts on this, and you've asked me for my opinion several times, so you're going to get it. No holding back."

"I changed my mind. Lie to me," Amelia muttered.

"Nope. And since I knew you'd protest and make excuses to not meet Marsali, now's a good time to tell you she's here. Hiii, Marsali," Izzy called, waving to someone behind Amelia. "Scoot," Izzy ordered in a low breath to Amelia.

Amelia gasped and turned, realizing Marsali Jones was indeed joining them. But what Izzy hadn't considered was whether or not their off-set connection would, well, get back to the set. If Amelia's colleagues found out about this, she would never live it down. "Okay, then. Strangulation it is," Amelia muttered to Izzy.

"Ladies, how are we this evening?" Marsali asked, moving with graceful intent toward their table.

Marsali looked as put together as always, dressed as she was in a bright sleeveless top and white skinny jeans. The coral color of her blouse brought out Marsali's tan and the many freckles that looked so charming.

"Great now that you're here," Izzy said, motioning to Amelia to scoot over to make room.

"Amelia, it's so good to see you again," Marsali said, tone sweet.

"You, too," Amelia managed to mutter, knowing Izzy wanted Marsali to sit beside her on the booth seat in order to block her only hope of escaping the train wreck Izzy had put into motion.

"Please, have a seat," Izzy added, raising one of her perfectly groomed eyebrows in Amelia's direction.

Amelia glared at Izzy but scooched over so that Marsali could lower herself onto the padded seat and settle in.

"Amelia, don't look so nervous. I won't bite," Marsali said.

Amelia pasted a weak smile to her lips and took in the other woman's fresh-faced appearance. Marsali Jones was not what one might expect in a professional matchmaker. Amelia guessed Marsali to be in her late twenties, but with minimal makeup and freckles galore, Marsali wound up looking not much older than a teenager. Combined with her long, curly hair, she looked way too young to be weaving people's futures together in the lifetime kind of way. How was this ever going to work? "Sorry. My dear friend Izzy kind of sprang this on me."

"No worries. Before I take you on as a client, I have to feel comfortable with your willingness to be matched. So if you're truly not willing and you don't want to give this a try, we'll just move on and have some nice girl talk. But before you say no," Marsali said when Amelia opened her mouth, "I hope you'll give me a chance, because I'm pretty darn good at what I do. Are you willing to share your story? Is there a particular reason you're pursuing—"

"Sperm banks," Izzy interjected. "Sperm that could come from *anyone*."

Once again, the young waitress returned at the most inopportune time and caught the last of Izzy's statement. Amelia watched as the girl's eyes widened just a tad before she smoothed her features and attempted a modicum of diplomacy, something Amelia wished Izzy could learn. Fast.

"Um, can I get you a drink?" the waitress asked Marsali.

"Iced tea, half cut, please," Marsali said, smiling at the young woman. "Thank you."

"Coming right up. I'll get y'all's order when I get back."

Amelia watched as the girl slid a weirded-out glance in her direction before she walked away. Amelia shot Izzy what she hoped was a silencing look. "Seriously? Will you please stop airing my business to the entire restaurant?"

"Sorry," Izzy mumbled. "But it's the truth."

"You don't have to shout it to the world," Amelia said with a groan.

"If you're that uncomfortable talking about it, how on earth do you think you're going to be able to *do it*, Meli? Where would you say the kid is from? Mars?"

"Okay, okay, let's… take a breath," Marsali said, calmly inserting herself in the conversation. "Amelia, tell me about you. Let's start there, shall we? I know the answers to some of these questions already, but it helps to ask them again to break the ice and get things rolling. Let's begin with, have you ever been married?"

Forced to endure the next hour or so of torture unless she was going to jump up atop the table and make a run for the door, Amelia resigned herself to the conversation about to take place. "No. I haven't. I… I was asked once but we were too young."

"And in response she sold everything she had, emptied her bank account, and left for Europe the very next day," Izzy added.

"So marriage scared you?" Marsali asked, her gaze searching.

Didn't marriage scare everyone? "I was eighteen and he was my first real boyfriend. And since then, I've been living my life," Amelia said to them. She hesitated to own her truth. Didn't want to face it because she'd never again experienced a love like that one and in the *twenty-three years* of dating since, she'd felt like a failure because of it. Like she'd given up her one and only chance and had been punished because of it.

"I see. That is young," Marsali said. "Have you come close to marriage since then?"

"No. Well, sort of, but… I found a ring and thought

he was close to asking me but then discovered him sleeping with my neighbor so…"

"I see," Marsali murmured as she took notes. "Would you say you're wary because of your experiences? Afraid of repeating them?"

"Definitely. She dates sporadically," Izzy offered. "And the moment they get serious, she bolts."

"I don't bolt, I simply refuse to settle," Amelia clarified. "If I feel someone is getting serious when I'm just not that interested, I end things before it becomes more complicated. There's a difference. Marriage shouldn't be about settling. Not if you want it to last."

"Fine, I'll give you that. But you're definitely settling if you do this whole *sperm* thing," Izzy said, thankfully lowering her voice, "without giving Marsali a chance. Just try it, Meli. What can it hurt? Other than a date here and there since you moved back to Wilmington three years ago, you've worked nonstop. At this point, I'd be surprised if you remember what men look like."

"Okay, okay, ladies, let's focus," Marsali said softly, earning their attention once more. "Amelia, I think it's clear Izzy wants you to be happy. We can agree on that, right?"

"I suppose," Amelia murmured.

"Well, I have some great guys in my database looking for equally great women. We have a lot of ground to cover, but if you agree, I'd love to set you up. You're how old?"

"Thirty-eight," she murmured, avoiding Izzy's gaze because of her upset with her friend. "Which is why time is of the essence if I'm going to be able to get pregnant at all."

"I understand," Marsali said in a soothing voice.

"And believe it or not, I have some guys feeling the same way. They've put their careers first and have reached an age where they want to be a father before they feel too old to enjoy the experience. So let's start with what you like in a man. What attracts you and makes you want to get to know them better?"

Amelia closed her eyes and took a calming breath. Marsali and Izzy couldn't make her do anything she didn't want to do. Answering a few questions wouldn't hurt. Would it? "I like… intelligence, being able to hold an articulate conversation. I like good looks and manners. Someone who knows how to treat a woman like she is more than an object to be used for sex or housekeeping duties."

"A man who appreciates his woman as his partner," Marsali murmured. "I like those qualities, too. They're getting harder to find these days but not impossible. What else?"

Amelia lifted her shoulders in a shrug. "He'd… have to be faithful. That's definitely a priority. I mean, if I'm involved with someone, I'm not just passing time until the next person comes along—and *that's* impossible to find in the dating world right now. I know," she stated, glaring at Izzy, "because I've tried to find that man despite what Izzy thinks, but men today say cheating is normal and everyone does it."

"Not true. Fidelity is hard to find but not impossible," Marsali countered. "It depends on where you're looking, and again, my database is filled with men who are actively looking for women who desire the same things you're describing." Marsali scribbled in her notebook and began making bulleted lists. "Does occupation factor in?"

That question threw her. She wasn't a snob but… "He'd have to bring something to the table. I mean, at my age, I have a home, a good job, a life. He'd need to enhance that, I suppose."

"No, you're exactly right," Marsali said. "You don't want someone who would be a detriment to your career. You want someone as motivated as you are and as successful. Someone supportive. Now, what about looks? Do you prefer facial hair? Dark hair or blond? Is bald or balding a yes or no?"

Amelia answered the questions one by one, even though she felt the whole process was useless. The waitress returned and took their order, and as soon as she was gone, Marsali picked up where she'd left off.

"What about kids? Okay if he has some already?"

"Yes."

"And you want children?"

More than anything. "Yes. If possible."

As the interview continued, Amelia found herself really thinking about her perfect match. Who he'd be and how they'd fit together as two parts of a whole. Marsali made it easy, gently leading her with another question when Amelia hesitated or helping Amelia narrow down too broad of an answer. They covered political stances and religion.

"What about pets? Are you a dog person? Cat only? What?" Marsali asked.

"Definitely no reptiles. Or rats," she quickly added, "or creatures of that sort. I'm allergic to cats so they're out as well. A dog would be okay."

"Dog-friendly is good. A lot of my men have happy, healthy dogs so it bodes well," Marsali said, smiling. "Okay. That about does it, I think. I have what I need from you, but I'll text or call you if I have any more questions. The good news is that I have a couple of men in mind," Marsali said.

"Seriously?" Amelia asked.

Marsali gave her a gentle smile.

"You're not demanding, Amelia. What you desire is a good man. An honest, loyal, hardworking man with integrity and drive. That's doable."

"If it's so doable, why haven't I met him already?" Amelia asked.

"Because they're working as hard as you are and go home just as exhausted. Plus, they have also been jaded by dating and have much the same reservations. Women aren't the only ones who have been cheated on and lied to, taken advantage of, and even abused. But they want to find someone special and are ready to commit, and know they probably won't find this person in a bar. Most of my clients are successful and therefore well-known in the area, and don't want their clients or associates seeing them on dating sites. That's why they go through me. It's discreet, the dates are vetted, and it's simply more professional. So, it's decision time. I can help you. The question is… do you want me to?"

Oh. Oh, boy. Even though Marsali seemed to be a wonderful person, this was a lot to consider.

Did she trust this process? Izzy was right in that Amelia's ways of meeting men hadn't worked, and she was embarrassed at her dating site fails, but a matchmaker? Really?

"I know that look," Izzy said. "Oh, Meli, come *on*. You have to do this. For me. For *yourself* and that baby you want so badly."

"I'm just not sure. Marsali," Amelia said, "I'm sure you're great at your job—"

"I am. My ninety-two-percent success rate is proof."

Ninety-two? "That's great. But you should know I've made an appointment and—"

"*At the sperm bank?*" Izzy said, her voice carrying to those at nearby tables.

"For the love of— Izzy, will you please *keep your voice down?*"

"No. No, I'm upset and I have every right to be. I won't let you do this, Meli. Friends keep friends from being stupid, and what you plan is *stupid*," Izzy said, shaking her blond head with enough force to rattle teeth. "You're giving up on love and romance and taking the easy way out. What if Marsali has the perfect guy for you? I know you're afraid of getting hurt again after wading through the sludge pit of men out there online, but if you're willing to go through a freaking sperm bank to get a baby, can't you *at least* give this a chance first? Give Marsali six setups. If they don't work, fine. Go do what you're so determined to do. But at least give Marsali a chance to find you the romance reset you so desperately need and deserve."

Amelia tilted her head to the side, and even though the conversation about men had been fun, it was time for a reality check. "Romance reset? Izzy, I'm not even sure I believe those men exist now. They're unicorns. Between porn, drugs and addictions, sexual deviants, and a few other *hard nos* for me, the odds are—"

"Ninety-two percent," Izzy and Marsali stated in unison, sharing a smile because of it.

Ninety-two-percent chance of finding a freaking unicorn?

Amelia stared across the table into her best friend's face. Izzy wanted to help her. Thought she was helping by setting this up and hiring Marsali. Was she ready for something like this? Because matchmaking was totally next level.

The first available appointment at the sperm bank was a little over four weeks away. Which, technically, gave her plenty of time to meet *a few* of the potential men Marsali might procure between now and then and prove her willingness to try if for no other reason than to get Marsali and Izzy off her back. Amelia felt the intensity of their combined stares and caved beneath the pressure. "Fine," she said, holding up her hands in surrender. "I'll agree to being set up. But not six of them. I don't have time for that. I'm working long hours and I have to be on set Monday and it's gonna be a crazy few weeks while they're in Wilmington filming."

"Five," Izzy said with a not-so-innocent blink.

"One," Amelia countered.

"One's just for practice. Three. Final offer," Izzy added, this time with a stern glare. "Come on, Amelia. You have *nothing* to lose and everything to gain by doing this."

"It works like this," Marsali said. "I match you and you go out. If you both agree to go out again, you do. If one of you says no, then we move on to the next match. I'll be honest and say it's usually the third or fourth match that tends to stick. As I get your feedback on the first date or two, it helps narrow things down a bit more and streamline the process."

Amelia inhaled and waited several long seconds before finally nodding. "Fine. I'll do it. I agree to being matched and will make a concerted effort—*but* when I go to that appointment next month," she said to Izzy, "*you* will not say another word about it."

Izzy lifted her glass and Marsali quickly followed suit.

"To doing it the old-fashioned way," Izzy said with a high tilt of her blond head.

"To good men," Marsali countered. "And may I find one quickly for Amelia."

Amelia clinked her glass against theirs. "To unicorns."

Chapter 2

"Better watch out."

Lincoln Hayes turned at the sound of his neighbor Mac Jones's deep voice and lifted his drink in a salute. "Hey. Nice party." Mac's house stood between Lincoln's and his brother Carter's house, and as the fairly new arrival to the neighborhood, Mac had hosted a gathering to introduce himself and get to know his neighbors.

"Thanks. But seriously, unless you want to wind up in her database, steer clear of my sister. Marsali is eyeing you and Carter like a kid in a candy store."

"Database?" Carter asked, turning his head to scan the crowd inside the spacious home.

Younger than Lincoln by five years, Carter had the same dark eyes and muscular build as Linc, but his hair had yet to lighten. Lincoln's wife, Jill, had always said the premature gray he carried looked sexy and distinguished, but Linc knew it came from becoming Carter's guardian at the ripe old age of eighteen. His younger brother had been a hellion before their parents had died in a car crash, and things had gotten a lot worse before they got better.

"Professional matchmaker," Mac said.

"Seriously? That's a thing?" Carter asked. "I thought you were joking when you said that earlier."

"Nope," Mac murmured, narrowing his gaze on his sister as she approached. "And my best advice is to scatter. Now."

Lincoln chuckled at the warning, but none of the men actually moved as Mac's younger sister closed in on them. Marsali Jones looked nothing like her brother. She was a good foot shorter, for one, and her long curls were the polar opposite of Mac's short crew cut.

"Nice party," the woman in question said as she joined their group.

"Uh-huh," Mac stated with a dubious glare at his sister even as he wrapped an arm around her shoulders and tugged her close for a sideways hug. "Guys, my sister, Marsali Jones, professional troublemaker."

Marsali glared at her older and much taller brother before sticking her hand out to greet them.

"Lincoln Hayes."

"Carter Hayes."

"Ah, the neighbors," Marsali said. "And all bachelors, I've heard."

"See?" Mac said, the word followed by a groan. "Marse, stop trying to match up my friends. Before long I won't have any single buddies left. Tonight is all about fun, not you adding to your client list."

Marsali smiled what could only be called an ornery grin and Lincoln found himself chuckling. The two definitely fought like brother and sister, much like his twin teenagers, who'd taken Carter's four-year-old daughter home from the party after an hour, citing boredom.

"What about you?" Carter asked, giving Marsali a once-over. "If you're a matchmaker, where's your ring?"

Lincoln wasn't sure if the question was out of interest or mere curiosity, but it brought a flush of color to Marsali's cheeks and a glare from Mac.

"No ring yet," she said simply. "But trust me when I say my skills at matchmaking are superb."

"Gotta give her that," Mac stated somewhat drolly. "She might be a pain but she has a ninety-two-percent success rate."

Lincoln was impressed by the percentage if nothing else. It was surprising given her age and sweet appearance.

"Marsali! Come here, girl, you have to meet someone," a woman called from across the room.

Marsali lifted her hand to indicate she'd be right there.

"Duty calls. Gentlemen, it was lovely to meet you. Mac, stop scaring potential clients away," she ordered, smiling at them before she left to join the crowd across the room.

"She's cute," Carter said.

Lincoln winced and watched as Mac glowered at Carter in typical older-brother style.

"Off-limits."

Carter grinned and Lincoln took hold of Carter's shoulder, tugging him away from the bigger, bulkier Mac. Sometimes he wondered if his little brother had the sense God gave him to steer clear of trouble rather than run toward it. "Haven't I taught you not to poke a bear? Buddy rule counts here."

"Exactly. Off-limits," Mac repeated, nodding in response to Lincoln's words.

After a hard look at Carter, their host excused himself to mingle.

"She is really cute. I could see her—"

"No," Lincoln said.

Carter laughed even as he took a drink.

"Fine. I'll go find someone else to hit on then."

Knowing his brother, it wouldn't take him long. Carter had a bad-boy look about him but tended to be a romantic. Carter seemed to attract the type of women who weren't looking for more than a good time. It had landed his brother married—and divorced—twice.

Thirty minutes later, Lincoln settled himself onto the patio furniture lining Mac's deck and took a drink from the bottle he held. A few people wandered around Mac's yard, looking at the newly designed landscaping recently finished by one of Carter's subcontractors. Thankfully the deck was quiet given the mugginess of the August night.

"Nice and quiet out here," a soft, feminine voice said from behind him.

Lincoln turned to find Marsali slowly moving toward him from the door she'd exited off of the kitchen. "Hey. Are you enjoying the party?"

"Yes. I didn't realize my brother was such a good host," Marsali said with a grin. "May I join you?"

"Sure." Lincoln stood as a good southern gentleman was taught to do when a lady joined him, and waited while Marsali curled up on the cushioned sofa opposite him before reseating himself.

"I, uh, noticed you were getting quite a bit of attention in there. Is she your girlfriend?"

Marsali's observation brought out a groan he couldn't control. "No. A married neighbor who's had a little too much to drink. I thought I'd hide out long enough for her husband to take her home."

"I see. Lincoln, I was wondering…"

Instant unease filled him. Had he escaped from one woman inside only to get trapped by another outside? The wound from Jill's death from a car accident was still raw in some ways. Between that and the deaths of his parents, not a day went by that he didn't wonder if he'd lose everyone that way. "I'm a widower, Marsali. Three years last May."

"Oh, I didn't realize." Her expression softened to sympathy. "I'm sorry for your loss. Mac simply referred to you three as 'bachelor row,' and I mistakenly assumed you'd never married or were divorced or something. How long were you together?"

"Fifteen years."

"That's wonderful."

He nodded, his thoughts going back in time. "We married young. I was twenty, working construction full-time, going to night classes to get into real estate, and raising Carter after my parents died. Jill was nineteen when we met in class. Those were some lean, hard years but we made it work."

The breeze off Carolina Cove's canal brought the scent of salt air along with the low hum of frogs and cicadas and a few boats slowly making their way back to the marina. As always, the scents and sounds brought peace and reminded him that life, however painful, moved on.

"Lincoln, I don't want to intrude but have you dated since then? I'm sorry, I know it's a personal question, and I don't mean to pressure you in any way. Truly. Just wondering if you've been feeling lonely?"

"I… Sometimes," he admitted even though he knew her reasons for asking. But maybe she could help him find someone to spend time with?

"Well, again… please feel no pressure, but I'm always looking for quality clients. It would be a great way to get your feet wet in the dating scene." Marsali flashed a brief smile. "You aren't the only professional who works long hours, and I'm guessing you've outgrown the bar and party scene. A lot of people find it hard to meet other singles, so I bring the singles to them after vetting them."

With the kids prepping for college and active with their friends, he'd thrown himself into work after Jill's death to combat the loneliness that snuck in when he wasn't on guard. But did loneliness mean he was ready to date? "How do you vet them?"

He asked more out of keeping the conversation going while he pondered his readiness, but he was curious, too.

"I do a full background check on each of my clients. Even a financial check if they allow it and it's requested. That's in addition to their one-on-one interviews, where I ask a ton of questions and generally assess them, keeping in mind potential matches from my database."

"That sounds… difficult."

Marsali grinned again and shoved her thick curls behind her shoulder. "Not at all. If you know what to look for. I have a background in psychology and constantly study personality tells. People give blatant clues as to their hang-ups, red flags, what have you. Most of the time, we daters ignore them and hope for the best, but a matchmaker picks up on those tells and works to either match them with someone suitable or we steer them toward whatever professional help we feel they might need, in the case of someone who's too insecure, has self-esteem issues, or problems with trauma."

"Do I remember correctly Mac mentioning something about you writing a book?"

"I did. It'll be released soon," she said, her expression revealing her excitement. "Very soon, actually. It's a guide for women and dating. So many women struggle with finding the right man, and my list of guidelines and rules, if you want to call them that, will eliminate some of the guesswork as to why certain couples simply don't work. Matchmaking is old-school, I know, but there's a science to it that is simply fascinating, and with the right matchmaker, things can go very well."

Lincoln smiled at her enthusiasm and love of her profession, noting how animated it made her just talking about her livelihood. "I see. Well, to answer your earlier question, no, I haven't tackled dating yet."

Marsali tilted her head to one side as she gazed at him, her expression not pitying but… knowing? Until then, Marsali looked like every other twenty something, but the awareness in her gaze left him changing his opinion to that of someone with an old soul, and knowledgeable about many things beyond her years.

Most everything had a science behind it, so he supposed it only made sense that finding that special someone would use some sort of formula as well.

"Lincoln, I can't imagine what you've been through, but I know getting back into the dating world is tough. Mac has said wonderful things about you. He thinks a lot of you, and after chatting with you, I get that same impression. If you're interested, I'd be happy to match you with someone. The first match is even on me. My treat. Here," she said, digging for and slipping a rectangle from her pocket, "is my card. It has all my numbers and my website, where you can check my background and qualifications. There's also free tutorials about dating, conversation starters, that sort of thing. You might find it interesting. Just so you know, my clients with children especially like the background check aspect and interview. It's a two-step way of weeding out the crazy that might slip through otherwise."

Lincoln took the card and nodded at Marsali. "Thanks, Marsali. I'll think about it."

"Good. I hope so. You seem like a good man, Lincoln. There are a lot of women out there searching for you."

He glanced at the card and lightly tapped it against his leg. "We'll see."

"Okay. Sales pitch over. I'll leave you be to enjoy this beautiful night."

Lincoln stood when Marsali got up and said her goodbyes. Once she headed toward the door to reenter the house, he moved off the deck, into the yard, to an even more private spot to ponder their discussion.

Lincoln turned and stared up at the three-story house fully lit up and bursting at the seams with Mac's neighbors and colleagues, remembering a time when he and Jill had played hosts for one reason or another during their marriage.

A wave of loneliness hit hard, and he wondered if it was due to his conversation with Marsali or the awareness the twins would be going away to college in a matter of weeks, leaving him to face the rest of his life alone. Maybe he should look into Marsali's services. At least check out the website and tutorials and brush up his rusty flirting skills. He definitely wasn't the type for bars or clubs. Never had been. That was more Carter's thing.

Lincoln focused on the familiar faces inside Mac's home. He had plenty of friends and colleagues in real estate, a few of them in that house, but no one came to mind when he thought of dating again. And he knew he wouldn't meet someone sitting at his desk or at home. But… was he ready? Was this what he wanted?

Lincoln stared at the house a bit longer before he decided to make his escape while he was free to do so. He walked next door to his home but the moment he opened the door, the emptiness hit him in a wave. The kids would eventually return tonight, but in a few weeks, that wouldn't be the case. The house would be as big and empty as it was now, night after night, and he'd have only the television for company.

He cleaned up the errant dishes in the sink, watched some television. Waited for the twins to return from Carter's house, where they'd taken Piper home from the party and started a movie.

His gaze shifted to the travel brochures he'd picked up on a whim as he'd passed by a display. He'd pulled them out of his computer bag earlier to empty it and then set aside the brochures because he didn't like the idea of traveling alone. Carter couldn't be away from Piper for long, and Mac stayed busy running his various businesses… There were Meetup groups dedicated to traveling singles, but traveling with a group of strangers didn't appeal either.

Lincoln pulled Marsali's card from the pocket where

he'd put it and called the number. Thankfully it went to voicemail, no doubt because she was still at her brother's party. "Yeah, Marsali, it's Lincoln Hayes. I thought about what you said and… I think I'd like to set up a meeting with you. I… Yeah. Let's do this. I'm ready to have some fun."

Chapter 3

"Why am I doing this?" Amelia asked two weeks later, staring into the mirror above her bathroom sink. "This is crazy. It's beyond crazy because it's *hope*less."

"The first time was a practice date," Izzy said from the other room, where she was sprawled across Amelia's bed.

Her friend had arrived an hour ago after dropping off a piece of her artwork for a downtown shop and claimed to be there for moral support. Amelia wasn't so sure that was the case. Because really? If not for her friend, she wouldn't be stressing about the hours ahead. Somehow going to a sperm clinic seemed easier than what was basically a blind date.

"The second time will be the charm."

"Isn't the saying the third time is the charm?" she muttered, her voice echoing off of the mirror in front of her. "Am I really going to have to go through this again?"

"I'm an optimist," Izzy said. "It'll be the second.

And you said yourself the first match wasn't horrible and he was a nice man, you just weren't attracted to him enough to go out again. Marsali gets that time is of the essence, so I'm sure this one will be better. Think positive!"

Amelia applied mascara and made that face women tended to make while doing so, her words coming out elongated and weird as she focused on the task and tried to tamp down the nerves churning in her belly. "What makes you think this one will be better than the last?"

The date Marsali had arranged hadn't been bad. The man had been polite and courteous, but she'd felt no chemistry whatsoever. It was like sitting across the table from one of her brothers. He'd stated repeatedly that he'd like to see her again, but she'd stayed noncommittal, even during the extraordinarily awkward good-bye, when he'd given her a kiss on the cheek. His interest had been clear, which made the evening all the more difficult.

"What did Marsali say about this man when she called you?" Izzy asked.

"She said he's tall, dark, and handsome, with a little salt in the pepper, thirty-eight like me, and in real estate. And he's a widower."

"Oh, ouch. Kids?"

"Two," Amelia said, giving up on the makeup and deciding it was as good as it was going to get. "Marsali never wants to give too much information because she wants us to have plenty to talk about in the get-to-know-you stage, so that's all I got from her beyond where we're meeting and such."

"Well, the tall, dark, and handsome part sounds

yummy. Just go and enjoy. Where are you having dinner?"

"Wrightsville Beach," Amelia said, naming the restaurant.

"Good choice. The view is amazing there. See? You're off to a good start already. It'll all work out."

"I don't know. I mean it," she said when she spotted Izzy rolling her eyes. "How crazy is it to go meet a stranger on what is basically a blind date when the news is full of sex traffickers?"

"Seriously, Meli? Marsali vetted him. He's not a sex trafficker—or a serial killer like you accused the last one of being."

"I didn't accuse him of anything. I just said *to you* that it was possible."

"Anything is possible these days."

"Yeah, that comment? Not helpful."

Izzy laughed and rolled to sit upright on the edge of the bed. Amelia glanced at Izzy and wondered how anyone as beautiful as her younger friend could still be single. Izzy was picky, though, and since Amelia had known her, a rare few men had ever made the cut and managed to get Izzy to the dating stage. Izzy typically cut them loose after a few days' thought for one reason or another, none of which ever really made sense to Amelia.

"You're nervous. I get it," Izzy said in a soothing voice. "Look, if it would make you feel better, I'll come with you."

"Be serious."

"I am," Izzy said, shrugging. "It's Friday night, I have no plans, *and* I just got a very healthy commission from the painting I dropped off earlier. I'm due some really good seafood. I could come with. We ride there, split up once we get there, I sit at the bar and have a nice meal while flirting with the bartender, and you do your thing meeting your date. I could use a dinner out, trust me. Doritos can only so many meals make."

"You'd do that?"

"And get to see one of Marsali's wonderful men from afar? Absolutely. I want to know if you're being too critical, and this is the only way I'll be able to judge."

"I don't know, Iz."

"Hey, just an offer. I'd keep my distance unless I see you head to the ladies' room. Otherwise I'll eat, drink, and flirt, and head out to the car after you send a text that the date is over. Or you could be nice and pick me up at the door. You'll never hear a peep from me, but I'll keep a discreet eye on you. Sound like a plan?"

"Yeah, it does, actually." Amelia hesitated at the thought of taking someone else on her date but gave in to the lure of security. A girl couldn't be too careful these days. And a background check wouldn't necessarily vet out crazy. Had they done this the first time, maybe Amelia wouldn't have been so nervous? Why were these setups so… difficult? *Maybe because you didn't instigate them?* But it would make her feel good to have a friend nearby. "Fine. I guess that means you're my incognito plus one."

"Yay! I need five minutes," Izzy said, grabbing her large purse. "Oh, and to raid your closet. Hey, if I'm going to sit at the bar, I might as well look good. Maybe I'll find a lonely Mr. Right."

"Maybe you should've hired Marsali to match *you* instead of *me*," Amelia said, her tone grumbling while Izzy proceeded to strip.

Amelia vacated the bathroom and pulled on the clothes she'd picked out earlier before taking Izzy's place on the bed. Izzy might be an artist and free spirit in some ways, but in others she was always prepared. That magical bag of hers held everything from makeup and sketchpads to a bikini and all the odds and bits Izzy might need to hop a flight or solve whatever problem might come up. Izzy had amazed at times, from producing whatever was needed for a wardrobe malfunction or a bad hair day to being passport ready on a whim.

"Oh, no," Izzy said, bringing Amelia's attention back to the present. "This is alllll you. I'm not the one Googling sperm banks. But just think, you still have four whole weeks left if you change your mind about your three-matchup rule. You know Marsali wants to help you, and she'd be happy to continue matching you until you find the one."

"You mean the one I don't believe actually exists?" Amelia pulled a throw pillow from the bed to hug and dug her toes into the carpet beneath her feet.

"Really? Are we going back to that again?" Izzy asked with the snap of her eye shadow palette.

Izzy turned and leaned a shoulder against the doorframe of the bathroom, her gaze so uncomfortably direct Amelia squirmed. "Why not?" Amelia said. "Izzy, that's why picking someone out at the sperm clinic might work for me. I mean, what are the odds that there is a perfect person out there for everyone? Or the odds that I'll actually find mine?"

"If you think of it that way, it is depressing, but I think there are *a lot* of someones out there we would be happy with, and the key is finding one of them. Those odds are better and it takes the pressure off, right? Because we're not searching for that perfect someone. We're going for someone we can be happy with."

"Isn't that settling?" It sure sounded like settling to her. Because even if there were multiple someones out there, finding one was still an issue. After all, there was a big, wide world out there with billions of people.

But, again, what if her high school boyfriend was her *one*? What if she'd walked away and, in doing so, set the course to be alone her entire life? Could she bring herself to settle for something less than what she'd had in the past? Because no one had ever compared to—

"No, it's not settling," Izzy argued. "Happiness is just… It's being content with what you have, including the person you've fallen in love with, who loves your good and bad, just like you love theirs, and focusing on making that relationship the best it can be. You work together, you're not at odds."

"Look at you getting all philosophical and romantic."

"Hey, I have my moments," Izzy said with a toss of her short hair. "All I'm saying is that we aren't fourteen-year-olds with our heads in the clouds dreaming of romance-novel romance. We've both seen the real world. Lived, loved, and *learned*. It's unrealistic to think it's gonna be sunshine and roses springing up out of the cesspit that is dating. But we *can* find love. Don't doubt that."

Amelia hated that Izzy made so much sense, but she couldn't deny the truth of her bestie's words. It *would* be a lot easier raising a child in a family atmosphere. Maybe she should stop being so negative toward the process and take it one date at a time? Heaven knew that would help, but it would also be so much easier if her biological clock wasn't ticking away like a finely tuned race car whipping around the track. "Fine. I'll try."

"Yay. I knew I'd win. Wait, you're wearing that?" Izzy narrowed her gaze and shook her head. "No."

"What? What's wrong?" Amelia asked, staring down at her clothes.

"You're too professional. Meli, this is a date. You want to be casual. Fun and flirty," Izzy stated, shoving herself off the wooden frame. "I'm going closet diving. Do you still have that skirt I gave you?"

"Yeah. But it's awfully short. You should've kept it and had it hemmed up for you." Izzy was about four inches shorter than Amelia's five eight, but they were the same size otherwise.

Izzy began digging and searching.

"Ah! Here it is. Put this on," Izzy said, shoving it at Amelia.

Amelia eyed the patterned beach-themed skirt and sighed. "I'm not going to win with this, either, am I?"

"Nope," Izzy said, her voice muffled by the closet as she dug for a blouse.

Amelia unzipped and shrugged out of the palazzo pants she had on and carefully laid them across the bed before pulling on the skirt. Thanks to the height difference, it landed a hair above mid-thigh. "Are you sure it's not too short?"

A blouse hit her chest and Amelia scrambled to catch it before it fell to the floor. Interesting. Not something she would've chosen to wear with the skirt, but the color combination totally worked. She'd have to remember this in the future.

"It's perfect. Especially with those stilts you call legs. Let's see you. Hurry up."

Amelia donned the sleeveless blouse, but before she could do much more, Izzy's fingers unbuttoned one of the buttons over Amelia's chest.

"Don't you dare button that back up. Oh, this is good. Much better. Now, jewelry. And perfume. Leave your hair a bit mussed. It's sexy."

Sexy? Amelia waited and let Izzy do her thing. Her friend moved to the dresser to look over the various items on display for easy access and chose a bracelet and dangly earrings. Finally, after a spritz of perfume on her pulse points, Izzy deemed Amelia ready.

"Remember. Now that Marsali has your feedback on the first date to go along with what you told her during your client interview, the odds are even higher that this will be the guy. Just enjoy yourself."

Maybe. Only time would tell.

While Izzy went back to the closet for something for her to wear to the restaurant, Amelia reclaimed her perch on the edge of the bed and waited. During her dinner with Izzy and Marsali, the matchmaker had bombarded Amelia with questions about her likes and dislikes, temperament preferences, pet peeves. No stone was left unturned, and Marsali did the same interviews with the men. Maybe this one would be better now that the first one was out of the way? But Marsali had no way of judging chemistry, so theoretically it could be another dud.

No. We're thinking positive. No duds!

"Okay, I'm ready. Oh! We forgot shoes for you.

Where are those new shoes of yours that I love so much? The wedges with the ankle straps?"

Amelia moved to the closet once more and found the shoes Izzy coveted. One of the perks of being on set so much behind the scenes was making friends with the costume designers and getting various castoffs at the end of filming.

Amelia donned the shoes, then took a deep breath before she stood and towered even higher over her shorter friend. "How do I look?"

"Dang, girlfriend. I'd totally date you. Now… what are we going to do?"

Amelia blinked. "Go to dinner?"

"Find a man!" Izzy said in her best cheer voice. "Let's do this."

Izzy had chosen a turquoise tunic Amelia typically wore with leggings, but given their height difference, Izzy was able to wear it as a dress. Paired with her blinged-out flip-flops, it looked cute and summery.

Traffic was thick due to the weekend and beautiful weather, and forty minutes later, Amelia dropped her friend off outside the restaurant to get herself situated at the bar before parking her secondhand Mercedes SUV in the lot. She took a final look in her mirror and touched up the lipstick she'd worried off during the drive.

Her heart pounded in her chest, and even though she'd done this once already, her anxiety skyrocketed. Meeting someone naturally at the grocery store or a park was one thing, but when she was so aware of it being a setup, she couldn't help but think it added another layer of stress.

Amelia got out of the vehicle and clutched her wrap

and purse as she headed toward the restaurant, aware of several male heads turning as she made her way to the entrance. At least her appearance was on point tonight and the admiring looks boosted her flagging confidence.

Like the first time, she paused at the hostess stand and gave Marsali's name. Marsali valued the privacy of her clients, and unless Amelia chose to give the man her full name and contact info, everything went through Marsali, including the dinner reservation.

"This way," a handsome young host said. "Follow me."

The young man's height and broad shoulders blocked her view as he led the way into the dining area, and Amelia's nervousness cranked higher, forcing her to take a steadying glance out the floor-to-ceiling windows at the beautiful view of the Atlantic beyond. The host stopped and Amelia stumbled a bit at the abrupt halt. She hoped her date didn't notice her clumsiness and think she'd arrived drunk.

She smiled at the host, who held her chair, before forcing herself to face her date for the evening. Amelia gasped sharply and practically fell into the chair when her legs gave out.

This couldn't be— Really?

Amelia stared into the black-brown eyes of Lincoln Hayes, all the while struggling to take a breath. Her body floated, transported back in time to the sweetness of first love and the heat they'd shared.

"Your server will be right with you. Enjoy your evening," the host said as he walked away.

Lincoln's eyes warmed, and the little lines at the corners crinkled as he smiled that gorgeous, make-her-knees-weak smile of his. Oh, he'd easily convinced her to do many things with that smile. Drag race in the dark of night on a deserted road, climb to the top of a water tower for a make-out session, fall completely and totally in love with him. So many things....

Except one.

"Amelia. It's been a long time."

Chapter 4

Lincoln slowly lowered himself into his seat at the table
and pondered the odds of his first professional match
being his high school girlfriend of two and a half years.

"It's good to see you, Lincoln. You look great," she
said, smiling.

"So do you."

Amelia showed little of the twenty years between
their last conversation—their breakup—and this one.
Her hair was still the same light brown, though now she
wore it shorter and curled along her neck and shoulders,
and her eyes were the same soft green with umber flecks
in them, reminding him of rich, thick moss. Amelia had
always had that girl-next-door look about her, but she'd
grown into a beautiful woman.

An awkward silence descended on them as they
stared at one another, gazes locked and searching. His
chest squeezed from the heaviness of the pain they'd
gone through, the pain she'd caused. And despite the
years, a bit of anger returned. No one liked getting
dumped, after all.

"Is this as… shocking to you as it is to me?" she asked.

"I—"

"Welcome. I'm Jamie. May I get your drink order?" a waitress asked as she paused by their table.

Since Lincoln already had a drink in front of him, Amelia ordered an iced tea.

"No wine?"

"Oh, I definitely need a clear head for this," she told him somewhat wryly.

Once the waitress walked away, Lincoln inhaled and nodded. "It is strange."

"Right? I mean, we dated twenty years ago but to match again now—"

She gasped sharply and Lincoln braced himself for whatever came next. Given her expression, it wasn't good.

"Marsali said you're a widower? Oh, Lincoln, I'm sorry."

He accepted the condolences with a nod and tried not to think of the grief that had lessened over the years but was and always would be there. "Thanks. It's been three years. Car accident," he said, since that was usually the next question. "She passed at the scene."

"Just like your parents."

Amelia's gaze softened even more and he saw a sparkle of tears she blinked away to keep in check. The sight touched him, though it confused him more. He wondered how Amelia could be so compassionate and yet walk away as she had. He'd lived in a fog afterwards, destroyed by Amelia's betrayal… until he'd met Jill.

"You've been through so much. I'm just… I have no words, Lincoln."

He nodded, not really wanting to talk about his life with his wife when he sat across the table from another woman who'd broken his heart with her refusal and disappearance twenty years prior. It was… weird, this boomerang feeling of time repeating itself. Except, this time it couldn't since Jill was gone.

"Lincoln, if this is too weird for you, I can go," Amelia said. "I… I know I hurt you, but believe me when I tell you I'm sorry for that. If it's any consolation, I broke my own heart that night as well." She glanced at the bar before turning back to him. "You know, I think I'm going to leave. You seem a little shell-shocked," she said, getting her purse from the chair beside her.

He watched her, told himself to let her go, but when she scooted out her chair, he stretched a hand across the table and placed it over hers, staying her. "We're here. Let's at least have dinner. For old times' sake. Okay?"

Amelia hesitated a long moment before she finally nodded and settled into her seat once more.

"So," he said, managing a smile at her. "Last I heard, you were backpacking across Europe and… dating some up-and-coming rock singer?"

His statement made her laugh, and Lincoln noticed several men turn to find the source of the joyful sound. It drew him, too, though he didn't like that it did.

"Oh, was that *ever* a long time ago. Wow. Yeah, I did that for all of a week, which must have been when I talked to whomever it was who told you. It was one of those things that sounded good when I called home, but the reality was quite different. I liked the shock value. My parents were appropriately appalled, but it didn't take long to realize I'd be one in a hundred girls."

"Good for you."

She shrugged. "I know it all sounds crazy, but it wasn't as alarming as I let on, trust me. We met hiking and he asked me to dinner, invited me to his concert. That's when I saw the chaos and knew it wasn't for me."

He found himself thankful she at least had the sense God gave her to know that about herself. It seemed as though girls now—even grown women—didn't know their worth and put up with far too much for far too long. His daughter sometimes mentioned the teen drama going on at her high school, and it made him crazy just thinking about it as a dad. As upset and angry as he'd been with Amelia at their breakup, he could only imagine how her parents had felt at her taking off the way she had. "And now? What do you do?"

"I'm a movie set designer."

"Seriously?"

"Yup. When I was traveling, I came upon a film set and managed to get hired as an extra. There's a lot of standing around and waiting as an extra, so I chatted up the designers behind the scenes. After that I was hooked and I worked my way through design school. One job led to another, and now I meet with production teams and pull together the sets needed for filming here in Wilmington. I've been doing it for the last three years or so since moving back to the area."

Lincoln watched as her expression changed in the telling. She definitely enjoyed her job. "And before Wilmington?"

"New York for a while, Hollywood after that, and then here. What about you? Marsali mentioned you're in real estate?"

He nodded. "Yeah. My life hasn't been as glamorous as yours."

"Trust me, it's not all glamour."

"Yeah, well, after you left, I stayed in construction to support Carter and myself. Once Carter graduated high school and began working, I started night classes. Real estate made sense since it was a short span to earn a lucrative license if you're willing to play the game and hustle. I've been doing it ever since."

Silence descended over the table after his statement, and he watched as Amelia glanced at the bar again. Maybe he shouldn't have phrased his statement the way he had, but how else should he put it? She'd left him, her parents, everyone. Plain and simple.

Since she still stared at the bar as though she wanted to bolt, he tried to take a casual glance. A blond sat at the bar talking to the bartender, along with a few other singles eating there rather than taking up a table. Why the fascination?

"Are you ready to order?"

While his attention had been focused on the bar, their waitress had returned. The too-chipper teenager reminded him of Breanne before her mother's accident. Since then, Breanne struggled with life and her place in it. Hopefully college would help her figure that out and bring back some of the sparkle now missing due to grief.

Amelia placed her order for a grilled chicken salad and he ordered salmon. Once the waitress walked away, the silence returned.

"Lincoln, I hope you've forgiven me for how I hurt you. I know I handled it badly and it wasn't right to do that to you. I just wasn't ready to get married and I wasn't mature enough to handle the breakup properly."

He nodded his understanding and realized had things been different, had she said yes, he wouldn't have had his children, or his life with Jill. "It worked out as it was meant to."

The words were easier to say now but hard to fathom back then. When Amelia had turned him down, he'd felt like it was yet another blow he wasn't prepared for. His anger after the breakup and the overwhelming responsibility of caring for Carter had left him feeling resentful. Especially when Carter acted out and, due in part to his grief, nearly wound up in juvenile detention.

"Tell me about Carter. How is he? And your children? How old are they?"

Lincoln took a long drink and settled back in his chair, the memories bombarding him. The tough times, the dark times, and then the good. "Carter is okay. He owns a lucrative construction company here in town that can pretty much build or subcontract anything needed. He's a single dad. His daughter, Piper, is four."

"Wow. Carter is a dad. I can't quite picture that."

He chuckled. "It's been an adjustment, for sure. Jill helped out a lot that first year, though. Eased the transition when his wife decided she didn't want to be a mother."

"Oh."

He nodded. He and his brother had definitely endured more than their share of heartbreak. Carter had taken their parents' deaths very hard. He searched for love but, after two marriages and two divorces, wasn't any closer to finding it. "My two are now eighteen and heading off to college in a couple of weeks, so they're staying busy packing up and saying goodbye to friends."

"Wait. Both of them?"

"Twins," he told her, nodding. "Brendan and

Breanne. Polar opposites in personality but similar in looks. What about you? Did you marry? Have kids?" The questions were hard to ask, even after all these years.

"Mmm. No to both. I worked a lot of hours while I went to school part-time. Then a lot of hours on various sets. I… fell in love again. Once. But I quickly discovered he wasn't going to give up dating, so that didn't work out. But, no, no ring and no kids."

She lifted her shoulders in a shrug that seemed casual but he sensed wasn't.

"Like you said, things work out as they're meant to, and obviously he wasn't ready to settle down so… better to find out sooner rather than later."

Their conversation continued as they got to know each other again. They caught up on parents and her many siblings, friends they'd kept in touch with since graduating high school.

Their food arrived and they dug in, their conversation shifting to more topics of favorite pastimes and local hangouts in and about town.

The dessert menu arrived when they finished, and even though Amelia shook her head, Lincoln found himself ordering a piece of chocolate cake with two forks.

Once the waitress walked away, Amelia narrowed her gaze on him.

"What?" he asked, feigning innocence when he knew he'd fail. "Chocolate cake no longer your favorite?" he asked, his mind shifting back in time to a parked car and a very private eighteenth birthday celebration he'd held for her on the north end of the island.

It was a good memory. A fond memory. One he hadn't thought of in many, many years.

Amelia's cheeks filled with color and she smiled at him. Lincoln found himself caught, snared by the look of her, sitting there across from him like nothing bad had ever happened. She was beautiful, talented. Familiar and yet not because she certainly wasn't the girl he'd known. She was… more intriguing as a grown woman? More tempting?

As his first date since meeting Jill, tonight hadn't been so bad—but after what had happened in the past, did he want it to continue?

Chapter 5

Dinner was delicious. The chocolate cake the best she'd had in ages with its delicious decadence. The conversation mostly easy and flowing until they came to the inevitable touchy subjects like his wife's death or Amelia's middle-of-the-night sprint from town and the emotions surrounding that fateful decision.

Amelia couldn't help but feel guilty. She should've better handled things with Lincoln. Talked to him instead of taking off and running away like a willful child. But at the time, she'd felt such pressure to accept Lincoln's proposal, and she knew if she stayed in town, she probably would've made amends and accepted his ring, tried to be the wife he wanted her to be instead of discovering the woman she was meant to become.

But what had she given up by leaving as she had? Her best child-bearing years were behind her and now… now there was no guarantee she'd ever have a child of her own, even if she went the sperm bank route. That was something she'd have to live with, one way or another. Would she be okay with never being a mother?

There were other ways, of course, but they weren't avenues she wanted to consider pursuing at this time, not without trying to have a baby first. She wanted to know what it was like. What it felt like to carry a baby, to grow life inside of her. To have something so intrinsically hers that it was flesh of her flesh and blood of her blood.

She blinked to awareness and realized they had both grown pensive, their laughter and conversation falling silent as they finished the shared piece of cake. She opened her mouth to speak but words failed her. What to say? What to do? How could she make up for the hurt she'd caused him?

"I don't know about you, but it's been a long week. Are you ready to call it a night?" he asked.

Honestly? She would've liked a walk on the beach or the pier. Anything to extend the evening just a little longer, because in her heart of hearts, she felt there wouldn't be another. "As you wish."

It was a quote from a movie they'd watched countless times while dating, and the mention of it now brought a slight smile to Lincoln's craggy features.

"Those were fun days. At least, I thought they were."

"They were, Lincoln. I've never regretted them. Only… what I did to hurt you. I'm truly sorry."

His jaw tightened at her words, but the waitress bringing their check ended whatever he might have said.

"Please let me get it?" she asked, reaching for the booklet with the slip inside.

"No." His reflexes were faster. "But thanks for the offer," he said.

Instead of a card, though, he paid in cash. So he

could make a clean getaway? Not have to linger while the girl ran the card and brought signature slips?

Lincoln scooted his chair from the table. "We should go. We've held the table long enough."

He couldn't wait to get away from her. That much was obvious. And it hurt like crazy. If this was any indication of how it felt when she'd left him, she couldn't blame him for wanting the night to end. He'd made good on the date. Been a gentleman as his mother would've wanted him to be, but now?

Amelia choked down the growing lump in her throat and led the way through the restaurant toward the door. She noted he didn't place his hand at her back as he'd always done. Another sign of his displeasure with her and how she'd injured him. Lincoln wasn't a player. Never had been. His love had been sincere, and she'd tromped on it like the ungrateful child she'd been.

When they reached the exit and were able to walk side by side she said, "I, um, wasn't sure about tonight. This whole matchmaking thing wasn't my idea but a friend's. It's a long story, but I'm glad it was you, Lincoln. I'm glad that we could talk and… I hope you'll forgive me for running out like I did. I would very much like a fresh start with you."

There. He couldn't misinterpret that now, could he?

"I'm glad you stayed for dinner, Amelia."

O-kay then. The roar of the waves crashing nearby and the sound of a Friday evening at the beach filled the air. Lincoln's cologne teased her nostrils, a mix of sandalwood and musk and something masculine and sniff-worthy that she couldn't identify.

Marsali's description of Lincoln was spot on. His hair was dark but light at his temples, with more than a hint of silver scattered throughout, close-cropped though it was.

Between becoming his brother's guardian at eighteen and now losing a wife with children to raise, she didn't doubt that accounted for the premature gray. It didn't detract from his looks in any way, though. In her opinion, it added to his allure, especially when he towered head and shoulders above her even with her heels, all broad and strong and formidable. She'd always been attracted to tall men, and Lincoln was definitely that. Lincoln was... everything, the whole package.

After they exited the building, she paused to remove the wrap from her shoulders. She'd needed it inside due to the chill of the air conditioning, but outside, it quickly became too much. Lincoln stood silently beside her as she fussed with it to buy time, hoping something might change between them. Maybe she should suggest a walk along the sand?

"Where are you parked?"

Yeah. Right. Okay, then. "Uh... that way."

They fell into step beside each other once more and her brain scrambled to find the right words. "Lincoln? I never mentioned you by name to Marsali. Did you mention me?"

"No."

"I just... I wonder at the odds."

He didn't comment, and she took a sideways peek at him to find his attention focused on the night sky above them. "I... I just wonder if maybe now that we're older and wiser, things would be different between us? That's me," she said breathlessly when he didn't respond, pressing the button on her fob to unlock the vehicle with a blink of the lights.

He moved to the driver's-side door and opened it for her but didn't lean down to kiss her or… anything.

"It was nice seeing you again, Amelia."

Amelia stepped toward him and lifted her face toward his, pushing and knowing she did, but more than ready for whatever Lincoln might propose as their next step. Coffee? Casual conversation? She just didn't want this to be the one and only time she ever saw him. "It was wonderful to see you, too. Maybe… we can do this again sometime?" Fine. If he wasn't going to say it, she would. Desperate-sounding or not.

Lincoln hesitated before he lowered his head, but instead of kissing her lips, he brushed her cheek.

"Drive safe."

Feeling deflated and defeated, Amelia got in the car and locked her door. She watched Lincoln walk away before digging out her cell to text Izzy. She glanced over her shoulder, but Lincoln had disappeared into the night and the assortment of vehicles parked outside the popular restaurant.

She took a moment to simply breathe before slipping a finger over her phone and tapping on Izzy's name. *You ready?*

Yes! Can't wait to hear all about it. Lah, I couldn't get a clear look, but that man seemed HOT!

Amelia pushed the button to start the vehicle and took her time pulling on her seat belt and cranking the AC. Her hands trembled throughout the process. She backed out of the space and approached the entrance of the restaurant, slowing to a crawl and then stopping when she saw Izzy merrily making her way down the steps and across the sidewalk. Izzy yanked open the door and hopped in, tossing her clutch, grabbing her seat belt, and turning sideways in the seat seemingly all at once.

"Tell me everything. Every single detail."

Amelia took a deep breath but struggled to form words over the stupid lump taking possession of her throat.

"Meli? What is it? Was he awful? You seemed to be enjoying yourself. I didn't want to stare but you laughed a few times. And he looked… well, he looked hunky enough. Was he awful?"

"N-no," she finally whispered, pressing on the gas to get them moving toward home. "He wasn't awful. He was… familiar."

"Familiar? You mean, you knew him?"

Amelia tightened her hands over the steering wheel and nodded. "It… turns out my date was… Lincoln."

"*What?*"

Izzy's shriek filled the car and blasted Amelia's ears.

"That was Lincoln? Lincoln Hayes *Lincoln*? The man you said you've always regretted letting get away, Lincoln?"

Amelia nodded, still battling that lump. Despite their ten-year age difference, she and Izzy had swapped heartbreak stories one evening over margaritas. Izzy knew all about Lincoln. Just like Amelia knew all about Izzy's men troubles.

"You mean to tell me that with the *thousands* of men in Marsali's database, she matched you with the love of your life?"

Her hands hurt because she gripped the wheel so tightly. "Lincoln hardly qualifies as that when it didn't work out."

"Yeah, right. Girl, you might be able to fool some

people but you can't fool me. I know how much you loved him. You can't hide it when you talk about him. And maybe it didn't work out back then but… what about now? When are you going to see him again? Please tell me you're going to see him again."

"He didn't… I don't know," Amelia said, rolling to a stop at a red light not far from the parking lot. "I panicked at first. I tried to leave right after I got there, but Lincoln was polite and asked me to stay. We talked a-about his wife—she died in a car accident like his parents, can you believe that?—and his kids. He seemed okay during the dinner, but… he didn't say anything about meeting up again when he walked me to my car."

"Maybe he just needs to think? It was shocking for him, too, I'm sure. I mean, it's good that he didn't just get up and walk out, right? He stayed for dessert," Izzy added as though that was proof positive things had gone well.

"My favorite," she whispered, nodding. "He remembered my favorite."

"Okay, see? He was surprised, just like you. He'll tell Marsali to set you up again, though. You wait and see. He will."

The light changed and Amelia pressed on the gas. It *was* a good sign that he'd stayed. Even better that he'd remembered her favorite dessert.

But if that was the case, why did her gut tell her she'd never see him again?

Chapter 6

The following afternoon, Lincoln sat at his desk in his home office and stared out the window at the boat traffic on the canal.

"Hey," Carter yelled from the first floor. "Music starts at seven. Leave around six?"

Had his brother never heard of texting? "Yeah. Sounds good."

Lincoln heard the door shut and went back to his deep pondering of last night's date with Amelia. She'd looked beautiful. The young girl he'd fallen so in love with had turned into an alluring woman who carried herself with confidence and assurance.

He wondered why she was single now. She shouldn't be. But then, he knew well that life didn't always work out as one planned. He'd certainly never expected to be a widower now. Over the years, he and Jill had talked about what they'd do when the twins went off to college. Travel, maybe take some classes together. Things that would help them focus on each other and their relationship sans kids.

His cell phone rang and he dug under the mound of papers on his desk to find it. A glance at the face left him frowning. His thumb hovered over the swipe bar, but he clicked the side to silence the ring and let it go to voicemail. He wasn't ready to talk to Marsali just yet. He had more thinking to do before giving his post-date responses as to whether or not there would be another date between them in his future.

He set the phone aside and tried once more to focus on the listing details in front of him, but as it had earlier, his mind wandered back to last night.

Amelia. Why hadn't she married? Why was she looking now? They were questions he wanted answers to, but there was only one way to get them and he wasn't sure he was willing to invest the time.

According to her story, she'd traveled for a while when she was young but went to school and settled into a career. Surely there had been plenty of opportunities for her to fall in love during that time. She'd admitted to coming close once but was that it? Only once?

Only one way to find out.

Giving up on the work in front of him, Lincoln shook his head and shoved himself away from the desk, deciding to join Carter and the kids downstairs. They were all in the pool and he could hear them splashing and laughing, and he didn't want to miss out. Not when, in a matter of days, his kids would be gone and the house empty. Some things took priority.

He changed into a pair of swim trunks and made his way downstairs, out the sliding glass door. Breanne lay on a lounge chair on her belly in a suit that made his head spin because it was so tiny, but Brendan, Carter, and Piper played a game of treasure hunt. Lincoln jumped in, close enough to the edge to splash his daughter and maybe get her to join in on the fun.

When he broke the surface and wiped the saltwater from his eyes, the lounger was empty and Breanne was shutting the patio door.

"Man, moody much?" Carter asked from the other end of the pool. "Pip, don't you turn into a girl on me, got it?"

"Okay, Daddy."

Lincoln frowned at the door where Breanne had disappeared until Piper swam over to him like the fish she'd turned into once she'd learned how to swim.

"Your turn, Uncle Linc."

He looked down at the brightly colored weighted pool toys she handed him and smiled at her. "My turn? Hmm. Let's see." Linc tossed two in the deep end and three in the shallows for Piper to dive for. While Brendan and Carter dove toward the deep end, Lincoln pretended to race Piper for the other three.

"Hey. Where were you last night?" Carter asked Lincoln after he surfaced with his prize.

Lincoln turned at the question but shrugged. "Kids were out, so I went to get dinner in Wrightsville."

Better to stick with the truth rather than lie. And omitting a few details Carter didn't need to know wouldn't hurt anyone. Especially when Carter would remember Amelia and all that had happened between them.

"I found two! I won, Uncle Linc!" Piper called.

"Good timing, Pip," Carter said to his daughter. "It's time to get out so I can get ready for the concert."

"Will you bring me back cotton candy?"

Carter laughed at the question and sliced through the water toward his baby girl.

"If the concert sells cotton candy, I think I can manage that," Carter told her. "No promises, though. Now let's get out so we can head home, okay? I want you out of the shower before the babysitter gets there."

After the group exited the pool, Lincoln swam some laps before doing the same. A quick shower and he was ready to go. He stopped by Brendan's room and heard his son's shower running, so Lincoln moved on to Breanne's room and knocked on her door. "Hey, sweetheart. We're leaving for the concert soon. I still have that ticket if you want to go."

"No, thanks. Let Bren bring another friend. I think Ty wanted to go."

Had she been crying? "Breanne, open up."

"Dad—"

"Open. Now."

A long pause followed, but he finally heard her moving across the room toward the door. She opened it a crack.

"What?" she asked, not looking directly at him.

"What's going on with you? Why the tears?"

"It's nothing, Dad. I'm fine."

His beautiful daughter was anything but fine. "Try again."

She rolled her eyes and shot him an irritated look that resembled Jill's so much he caught his breath.

"Jax and I broke up. But it's no big deal. It's not like we can date when he'll be in California and I'll be at Duke."

Young love was tough. He knew that from experience.

Lincoln reached out and tucked a wet clump of hair behind her ear. "Are you sure you won't come with us tonight? Nice chance to hang out with your old man, hear some good music."

"You're not that old. But no. I'm going to find a movie and hang out here with ice cream."

He smiled at the image, because anytime Jill had a bad day, a hug and ice cream were the cures. "You're sure?"

"Yeah. Have fun."

She tried to close the door but he stopped it with his hand. When she made eye contact, he took a step back and opened his arms, palms out and fingers wagging for her to bring it in. He got another eye roll for his actions, but she slipped through the door and hugged him. He squeezed her tight, taking the opportunity to kiss the top of her head. "It'll be okay."

"I know. It just bites."

That it did. He held tight for several long moments, not about to be the one to let go until he had to. Breanne pressed her face into his chest and then pushed him away.

"Night, Dad."

Lincoln watched as she stepped back into her bedroom and shut the door, wishing he could take away the pain he knew she felt. Much like him and Amelia, Breanne and Jax had dated since their sophomore year, and as boyfriends went, Lincoln couldn't fault the kid. The boy had drive, potential. And had received both an athletic scholarship and multiple academic ones to Stanford, giving the kid a full ride. Lincoln just hated that his daughter was experiencing the same pain he had at her age.

Lincoln still mulled over his dark thoughts of the past forty minutes later when they piled into Carter's Jeep for the ride to the amphitheater. Carter had removed the top and doors, and his son and two buddies sat squished into the back.

The drive took longer than expected due to traffic snarls, but finally they found a spot and grabbed their chairs from the rack on the back of the Jeep before making their way to the lawn.

"Dad, we're going to go on down front and see if we can squeeze in."

"Don't be rude," Lincoln ordered. "Come back if you can't find a spot."

"Okay."

The boys disappeared into the crowd, and Lincoln and Carter settled along the back of the lawn with chairs and a cooler of drinks between them.

"You seem awfully preoccupied," Carter said once they got situated. "Breanne okay?"

"She and Jax broke up."

"Ahhh. I wondered why he wasn't at the pool hanging out today. Tough break. Bound to happen, though, with him going so far away for school."

Lincoln's cell rang where it sat atop the cooler, and Marsali's name appeared.

"Whoa! Why is Mac's sister calling you?" Carter asked, his gaze narrowing suspiciously. "How does she have your number? Are you *seeing* her? Does Mac know?"

"I'm—"

"Ah, man. He pulled me aside *twice* the night of your party to warn me off, and here you're the one who went after her." Carter's chuckles drew the attention of those nearby. "That's funny."

"It's not like that."

Carter's chuckles died down after Lincoln's tone settled in.

"Well, if it's not like *that*, what is it like?"

Confession time. Lincoln supposed there was no time like the present. "I… might have hired her."

Lincoln struggled to keep his cool in light of Carter's smirking expression.

"Seriously?"

"Don't."

"Yeah, no, I *have* to. You actually did it? Hired Marsali to find you a date? Why not just go online?"

"Because I don't want clients and colleagues seeing my picture online like some— Can we not talk about this?"

"Show hasn't started yet. Nothing better to do." Carter took a long drink from his bottle and shrugged. "I guess that's smart, though. Online dating isn't great anyway. Same people on all the sites, and you have to wonder if they ever get off even if they wind up dating someone."

Lincoln didn't comment but that was exactly what he didn't want. Who would? He supposed there were those who wouldn't care because they weren't online for a serious relationship, but he wasn't the type to share. Some things were meant to be private and that definitely included relationships.

"I'm just glad you're finally dating. Seriously. You put the kids first and mourned Jill, and that's exactly what you should've done. But it's time to move forward.

Have you gone on a… Whoa, is *that* where you were last night? How was it? What happened?"

"You sound like Breanne and one of her friends," Lincoln grumbled.

"Who cares?" Carter asked with a grin. "I wanna know. Did you like her? Was she pretty? Where'd you go?"

"Yeah, yes, and Wrightsville, like I told you."

"Could you be a little more vague? Come on," Carter demanded. "Was it a bad date? Cut yourself some slack. You're out of practice, sure, but it couldn't have been that bad. Unless you're just being nice about the pretty part?"

"It wasn't bad," Lincoln said, shaking his head at Carter's question. His brother could be a little short-sighted sometimes. "It was… It was a great date except for—"

"What? Don't leave me hanging, Linc. What happened?"

"Marsali arranged the date, right? So I knew very few details beforehand. I got there and the date Marsali arranged was with Amelia Porter."

"Amelia… your old high school girlfriend?"

Lincoln nodded. "She's not old."

"She's still hot, huh?"

And then some.

"Wow. What are the odds?" Carter asked, scratching his head. "Yeah, I don't care if I sound like a teenage girl. I want details." Carter sat forward in his camp chair, staring intently at Lincoln while he waited. "Don't leave anything out."

Lincoln knew avoiding the conversation was futile, especially when he had nowhere to go with the concert about to begin, so he filled Carter in, starting with the gut-wrenching surprise he'd had finding Amelia at the table, to the fact her legs looked a mile long in that skirt and those heels.

"So she's back in town and looking… and you're looking. And low and behold your"—Carter lowered his voice—"*matchmaker,*" Carter said with a wide grin, "hooked you up as being compatible."

"I guess so."

Carter's gaze narrowed at Lincoln's tone.

"When are you going out again?" his brother asked.

Someone on stage began a rapid drum beat. Lincoln focused his attention on the concert venue and thanked God for the band assembling on stage and razzing the crowd to get to their feet. Guitar riffs filled the air and blasted the crowd, and Lincoln and Carter stood with the rest of the audience as the lead singer approached the mic.

Standing shoulder to shoulder with his brother, Lincoln said, "We're not."

"... Carter."

Chapter 7

That same evening, Amelia propped her feet up on the coffee table in her enclosed sunroom, her phone on speaker beside her on the cushion. "Wait, so you haven't been able to reach him?" she asked Marsali.

"He is a busy man, Amelia. No worries. I wasn't able to reach you all day either."

Right. Okay. "Yeah, I'm sorry about that. I had a tough day on set with a bunch of last-minute changes."

"Exactly. Remember that he's in real estate. I'm sure he probably had showings or open houses today. There's no need to panic. Unless…"

"Unless what?"

"You tell me. Did something happen?"

Confession time, Amelia mused. "Well… actually, yeah. I mean, sort of."

"Sort of?" Marsali repeated. "That sounds a bit ominous. *Did* something happen between you or not?"

"Marsali, Lincoln and I have actually dated before. In high school."

"Oh! Wow. I wasn't expecting that. I thought maybe

there had been an issue at the restaurant or something. So you dated in high school? For how long?"

"Almost three years. Lincoln, um, proposed to me and—"

"*Oh.* You mean *he* was the one you referenced when you said you almost married but were too young?" Marsali asked.

"Yes."

"Okay. Well, I have to say this is a first for me. I've never had this happen. Okay, so you have a history, but that was a long time ago. Tell me more about last night. Did you exchange any angry words? Did you talk about the past? Gain any closure?"

Amelia closed her eyes and relived the evening with Lincoln. The sight and scent of him, the way he smiled, the lightly callused look of his hands, which made her think he still did quite a bit of labor himself when he could. "He seemed okay, at least at first. We did talk about the past. I apologized for not handling it more like an adult. He said it worked out as it was meant to because he wouldn't have his kids. It went well, I thought."

"But?"

"But," Amelia repeated, "you haven't been able to get in touch with him for a follow-up, and when he walked me to my car and I mentioned how much I'd enjoyed the evening and made it clear I'd like to see him again, he didn't ask for a repeat."

"I see. Did you hug? Kiss?"

"He kissed my cheek."

"Did you feel chemistry with him?"

A flush of heat rose in her cheeks. "Yes." When she closed her eyes, she could still feel his lips on her skin, the sweet, fiery trail left in their wake, and the way his cologne had filled her head and teased her senses.

"And you'd be interested in seeing him again?"

"Only if he's willing."

"Of course. Obviously there was a lot of emotion tied to your early years together," Marsali stated, "but how awesome is it that the chemistry you shared is still there?"

"It was for me, but I'm not so sure that was the case with Lincoln."

"Time will tell," Marsali said. "And as soon as I know more, so will you. What you are going to do now is hang tight while I track him down, and we'll go from there. No worries, okay?"

"If you say so."

Marsali changed the topic to more general subjects before they said goodbye and Marsali ended the call. Amelia was tired but not sleepy, frustrated with not getting any feedback from Lincoln regarding their date, and wondering if he did actually hate her after all of these years.

She twisted sideways and flopped back on the couch, groaning aloud. "Why him? Why now of all times?"

Why did she think it was twenty years too late?

LINCOLN WAS VERY WELL aware of Carter's inquisitive stare at various times throughout the concert, but somehow his nosy little brother managed to keep his peace until the band took an intermission. The moment the music stopped, Lincoln turned toward Carter and said, "Don't start."

"Since when did you saying that ever stop me?"

Carter said with a wide grin. "Why aren't you seeing her again?" he demanded, picking the conversation up as though the last hour hadn't happened.

Lincoln lowered himself into his camp chair and leaned forward to pull a cold water bottle from the cooler. "I have my reasons. None of which I want to share with you."

Carter continued to glare at Lincoln.

"Wow."

Lincoln knew better than to ask. Told himself not to but asked, "What?"

"Twenty years later, you're still in love with her."

Lincoln inhaled and released a heavy sigh. "I am not in love with her."

"Fine. Maybe *in love* is a bad description, but you never got over her. Admit it."

Lincoln opened his mouth to deny the statement but the words wouldn't form. "I loved Jill."

"No one's saying you didn't. But seeing Amelia again wouldn't have freaked you out this much if there wasn't something still there."

Lincoln busied himself by taking a long pull from the water and hoped it helped the August heat and the intensity he felt because of their discussion. "I've made up my mind. I'm not going to see her again, Carter. Drop it."

Carter sat back in his chair, and neither of them spoke for a long moment.

"I remember having a huge crush on her. Like, huge. I was so jealous when I'd catch you two making out."

"Why do you think I let you catch us?" His cell buzzed again and Lincoln pulled it from his pocket to glance at the caller ID.

"Marsali again? Answer it. You gotta talk to her sometime, man," Carter said.

Yeah, he did. But not here. And definitely not with Carter listening to every word.

Without warning, Carter smacked his hand under Lincoln's. The phone flew up in the air. Carter grabbed it and swiped to answer in a lightning-fast move.

Lincoln scrambled out of his chair, but Carter dodged him, as agile as ever.

"Marsali, Carter here. Lincoln's afraid to talk to you because he's still hung up on Amelia. Don't let him off the hook. Set them up again, okay?" Carter said, battling Lincoln's attempts to take possession of his phone. "Yeah. No matter what he says, he'll be there. I'll make sure of it."

"Give me that," Lincoln said, finally managing to get the phone away from his brother. Lincoln glowered at Carter, his hand so tight around the phone he heard the case crack. "You're dead."

Carter grinned. "Just doing you a favor."

A favor? How was he going to explain things to Marsali now?

Carter stood there beaming like the lunatic he could sometimes be, and Lincoln walked away from his brother with a low growl as he raised the phone to his ear. "Marsali, it's Lincoln. I'm sorry about that. We're at a concert and… let me get out of the crowd to talk."

"Take your time," Marsali said, her sweet voice filling his ear.

Lincoln moved to the back of the gathering where he could pace since he had a tendency to do that whenever he had to discuss something stressful. "Okay, so…

yeah. I'm assuming you've already spoken with Amelia?"

"I have. She explained that you two have a history. That's the first time that's happened to me but I'm not surprised. You two match very well on paper. As soon as you called me to give me the go-ahead to set you up for an interview, I knew you and Amelia would be a good fit."

"Yeah, well, I'm… not so sure that's the case."

"Amelia said the date went well once the initial surprise wore off. You don't agree?"

He swiped a hand over his face and rubbed hard but the tension remained. "The date was fine. It's just…" Marsali waited for him to finish, but her silence didn't help Lincoln form an acceptable excuse.

"Lincoln, first dates are always hard, and I imagine this one was doubly so with you coming out of mourning only to find Amelia there. Before you say anything else, let me ask a few questions. Did you have fun? Enjoy yourself?"

He inhaled and sighed. "Yeah. I suppose I did for the most part."

"Were you still attracted to Amelia? Have chemistry?"

He pictured her in his mind, her long legs and that skirt and the way she smiled up at him. "Yes."

"Okay. So far so good. My next question has to be, have you forgiven her for what happened twenty years ago?"

"Forgiving and forgetting are two very different things, Marsali. Amelia didn't just end our relationship, she packed her bags in the middle of the night and took off without another word. I needed her. Even if we didn't get married right away, I needed her. I'd just lost my parents, was given guardianship of Carter so long as I could show a stable home life for him, and she nearly wrecked all of it."

"Did you lose Carter?"

"No, but—"

"If you had stayed with her and lost Carter anyway, would you have blamed her?"

"Of course not."

"Okay, so if that's the case, what about what happened after she left? You met someone, fell in love, and married. If you had the chance to do things over again, would you change the path you took because Amelia left?"

He pinched the bridge of his nose and counted to three. "Marsali, I'm not giving you excuses. They're reasons why she isn't trustworthy."

"Few eighteen-year-olds are trustworthy, Lincoln, and from what you said, she was under a lot of pressure. In speaking with Amelia, I know she had a lot on her plate from a young age with her parents and siblings."

Lincoln's argument faltered and shattered into a fast death because Marsali was right. Amelia was the eldest of seven kids in a working-class family. She'd cared for her siblings since they'd been born, sacrificing after-school sports and friends and fun due to duty and responsibility. Even dating her had been an issue because it meant she could only go out if one of her parents was home.

And then he'd wanted her to marry him and take on him and Carter.

He'd been overwhelmed at the time. So burdened by all that had happened he hadn't looked at things from her perspective. As an adult, as a parent, now he understood the weight of what he'd asked of her. He also knew that he probably could've talked her into accepting his proposal if given more time, which was no doubt why she'd been so desperate she'd… run away?

Wait.

It was *his* fault? How had he not seen things from her perspective? Was he that much of a schmuck back then to think she should give up her life for them?

"Lincoln?" Marsali asked. "Are you there?"

A breath huffed out of his chest as the reality of the past sank in along with the present. Free. Twenty years later, they were both free to do as they pleased. Start fresh. If they wanted.

Would things be different now?

"Lincoln? Hello?"

"Yeah," he said, shaking himself out of the storm in his mind. "I'm here. The, uh, band is getting ready to start back up but I… I think I would like to see Amelia again after all. If she's willing."

"You're sure? I don't want there to be any misconceptions here. If you'd rather not, I can set you up with someone else, but once you pass on another date with Marsali, you understand you can't go back?"

"No, I understand. I'm sure. I want to see her." He had to see her again, if for no other reason than to own up to his mistakes and set the record straight now that the fog had cleared from his brain. He couldn't imagine Breanne taking on such a thing at her age, and yet that's what he'd expected of Amelia.

"Oh, good. That's great news," Marsali said. "I'd be happy to arrange things. Do you have a particular date idea in mind?"

Chapter 8

"You're seeing him again?" Izzy said the following week, her voice muffled. "Awesome. See? I told you to give Lincoln some time and he'd come around."

"You sound weird. What are you doing? Are you in a tunnel, and if so, why?" Izzy had done some crazy things in the years Amelia had known her, all for her art and the attention it would bring to the causes she held so dear.

Amelia pulled out yet another blouse from the rack and wished her friend was here to give her clothing advice again. Everything she saw in her closet sucked, and she wondered what had possessed her to purchase them.

"Um, is th-that better?"

Amelia paused and listened intently. What *was* Izzy doing? "Yeah, but you still didn't tell me what's happening over there. Are you home? On the island?" Another long... Were those pants? Not the wearable kind but the kind that came when two people were... "*Izzy*? Is someone with you?"

"I really have to go, Amelia."

Oh, really? "You can't," Amelia said, instilling all the desperation she could into her voice. "Izzy, I need help picking out an outfit, and since you got me into this, you have to help me. Don't you dare hang up," she ordered with a grin, wondering how long she could keep Izzy on the phone while her friend did whatever it was she was doing. Paybacks were, well, *that*, after all.

"Um."

"No excuses. You *have* to help me. I can't do this without you," Amelia added, struggling to keep the laughter out of her voice.

"Meli, you look great in everything."

"That's not what you said last—"

"Oh." *Gasp.* "I *really* have to— Bye!"

Izzy's goodbye emerged high-pitched and decidedly breathless, and Amelia's eyes widened as the phone clicked in her ear. She tossed it atop the bed, laughing at her friend's antics.

Well, well, well. Izzy could be doing something weird like crawling through a tunnel creating an art piece she didn't want to discuss because she never wanted to "lose the magic of creation," but she was also a fairly free spirit, which meant any number of other possibilities. Had Izzy met someone? And if she had, why hadn't she shared this info?

Focus on you. Hello? Time is running out.

She glanced at her watch and groaned before flipping through her clothing at a faster rate.

Marsali's instructions had been to dress casual. But how casual? It was a date, after all. And evening. A hot, muggy August evening in the south. She'd melt in the heat but get potentially cool in the muggy breezes. Decisions, decisions.

She inhaled and turned toward the opposite side, sliding through her clothes there. Examining, discarding, and wondering how one could own what she did and hate absolutely everything.

Stop letting your nerves get you. You wanted a second date and got it. That's all that matters. One step at a time. He's not going to care what you wear.

But how could she not let her nervousness impact her mood when she was so aware of the fact Lincoln had had no intention of seeing her again after their first date? She'd learned to trust her instincts over the years, and when Lincoln had left her at her car that night, she knew he had no intention of seeing her again.

What had changed his mind? Would he change it again? Was she getting her hopes up only to have them crushed later on? "*Auuuugh!*"

She closed her eyes and forced the what-ifs away. Tonight she had a date with a very handsome man whom she liked. End of story. No projecting what the future might or might not hold. Besides, she had a backup plan if things didn't work out.

But the thought of having Lincoln's baby?

"Stop, stop, stop," she ordered, opening her eyes and grabbing the next piece of clothing that came to hand.

This. She'd wear this. Well, maybe not.

Unless… She eyed the sleeveless romper with a critical stare. It did showcase her long legs, and Lincoln had *always* liked her legs. But she was meeting him at the marina, which meant there was a boat involved. Regardless of whether it stayed docked or not, the breeze on the water could be cool.

She turned to survey the rest of her closet with desperate eyes and spotted a lightweight duster that might give her just enough protection from the wind. It paired well with the romper and would add a little dramatic effect. She scrambled to find shoes, another pair of wedges that added to her height, and once dressed, she took a look in the mirror.

Yeah. That worked.

A classic song came to mind and she smiled. *She's definitely got legs.*

An hour later, Amelia parked her SUV at the marina and took a deep breath. No pressure. No expectations. No thoughts of the future or babies. Not tonight. Tonight she wouldn't think about her age or upcoming appointments or anything else. She would stay in the moment and simply breathe.

She exhaled slowly and swung her legs out of the vehicle, only then remembering to grab her bag and the duster lying in the seat beside her. Once she had those in hand, she got out and locked the car with a press of the key fob.

She had to slow her steps as she walked toward the boats bobbing up and down at their moorings. The little rocks atop the asphalt shifted randomly beneath her four-inch wedges and left her very aware that a slip and tumble would not be a good way to start a date.

Finally she made it onto the planks and searched the area for Lincoln as she slowly walked down the length.

"Hey, beautiful."

She turned at the sound of the male voice but found a very sun-grizzled and drunk man.

"You're looking for me, sweetheart," the man added, grinning. "Come join us."

The friends with him chuckled, and she turned away with a silent shake of her head and bumped nose to chest into Lincoln.

"She's with me," Lincoln stated firmly as he wrapped an arm around her to steady her. "Sorry, boys."

Lincoln steered her back up the ramp the way she'd come and across the way to another. Neither of them spoke until they were out of earshot of the group of men.

"I saw you drive in but wasn't in time to meet you before you'd headed the wrong way. Sorry about that."

Amelia liked the feel of his hand at her back, riding just above her hip. It was a show of protection and possession, both of which sent a tingle of pleasure up her spine. "All good. Which one is yours?"

"The *Pearl*."

"After your mother." Sweet. But then Lincoln had always been sweet. She remembered the night his parents had been killed. The night she'd spent cradling him as close as he would let her as he stared into space and tried to process the news while Carter slept upstairs.

Lincoln hopped aboard the *Pearl* and held out his hand to help her cross. She caught him looking at her long legs and her body warmed. *Good choice.* "So are we staying here? Eating onboard?"

"Nope. We're heading out, and before you ask where, you'll see soon enough. As much as I like the sight of you in those shoes, though, you might want to remove them. Save an ankle or two."

So they weren't taking the boat to a restaurant? Okay then.

Amelia settled herself in the chair behind the high

windshield beside Lincoln after he loosed the vessel and started the powerful engine. She donned the duster she'd brought with her as they trolled slowly out of the marina and into the Intercoastal, where Lincoln increased speed.

The wind made it difficult to talk without practically yelling, but the silence wasn't uncomfortable. She stared out at the passing scenery, the beautiful homes and lights that looked so serene in the setting sunlight.

There was something about being on the water. Something natural and freeing yet primal. The sights and sounds and smells cleared her mind of worry and wondering what the future would hold, blew away all but the moment at hand and the occasional whiff of Lincoln's sandalwood cologne.

Lincoln handled the expensive boat with careful precision, his hands practiced and steady. She remembered those hands touching her many years ago, and the memories brought another flush to her cheeks. Hot-blooded teenagers would be teenagers, after all.

She turned away from him to stare out once more, only then becoming aware of the boat slowing as they approached an isolated stretch of Masonboro Island.

Her nervousness suddenly kicked into gear once more. As dating teens, they'd bummed a lot of boat rides out to the uninhabited island. It was the best place to shell hunt and sun and party without the adults getting judgmental. But now there were no parties. No lights. No people. What were they doing here?

Lincoln anchored the craft with the expertise of an experienced boatsman. The only problem was they were still quite a ways from shore due to the size of the vessel, which meant—

"Don't worry. I've got you," Lincoln said in that deep voice of his.

He jumped into the water and carried two huge backpacks toward shore. Once those were safely on the beach, he returned and held out his arms, waving his fingers for her to jump.

Amelia laughed, glad she'd taken off her shoes earlier when he'd told her to. She tied the loose ends of the long duster around her waist to keep it from getting wet. She held on to the railing as she stepped over the side, getting her balance before she jumped, and even though she didn't mean to, she shrieked when Lincoln caught her. His chuckle warmed her ear and sent a sizzling tingle racing through her, making her tremble.

Lincoln cradled her high against his chest as he waded through the water, and in moments, her feet hit the sand.

"Hang tight while I change out of these wet clothes."

He pulled something from one of the backpacks and moved into the darkness toward a dune. Despite having seen it all before, she turned her back on him, toes digging into the sand at the effort he'd already made for their second date. Men like Lincoln... Well, she was grateful for a second chance. She wouldn't blow this one.

"Think you can manage one of these?" he asked moments later, handing her one of the backpacks.

She took it and knew it had to be the lighter of the two given the way his muscles bulged when he lifted the other. "Yes. I've got it."

"Good. Ready?"

He grasped her hand and led her away from the

beach, toward the interior, following a barely visible trail toward the center of the narrow expanse. Lincoln warned her of rough patches along the way and even grasped her waist and lifted her and the pack over a couple of spots to protect her bare feet.

Lincoln's broad shoulders filled the space in front of her, so she focused on their clasped hands and putting her feet where he treaded. When he stopped and stepped to the side, she gasped at what she saw in the fading light of the day. He'd... Wow.

There. Away from the water and tide that would wash it away was a pit with a stash of wood at the center, surrounded by a circular sand bench. Just like the one Lincoln and Carter, along with a group of friends, had dug that last perfect summer day before Lincoln's parents had been killed and their lives had imploded.

Tears stung her eyes at the sweetness of it. Leave it to Lincoln to remember her comment after that day that she couldn't wait for them to return for a picnic—just the two of them. "I can't believe you did this."

"I can't take all the credit. Carter, my kids and their dates, and I dug it out a few months back for the twins' graduation celebration. Thankfully it's stayed pretty much intact," Lincoln said, taking the backpack from her shoulder to dig inside. "I brought the wood out earlier today and fixed what needed fixed."

From the backpack she carried, he produced a couple of blankets and small pillows along with a lighter, portable speaker, and bug repellant coils and candles. He lit everything meant to be lit, then opened the second, larger backpack, which held a cooler with bread, cheeses, fruits, crackers, and tiny bottles of wine along with stemless wineglasses. She watched the process with dazed appreciation. "You've thought of everything."

"Not yet."

Lincoln removed his phone from a pocket, and with the press of a few buttons, soft music filled the air.

"But maybe now. You hungry?"

She laughed softly and nodded, accepting his hand for the two steps down into the pit. Amelia spread the blankets for them while Lincoln poured the wine and uncovered the prepared food. Finally they settled in beside each other, and Amelia broke the silence with the thought plaguing her. "This is above and beyond, Lincoln. I love it. But I'm surprised, too. I… wasn't sure I'd see you again after our first date."

Lincoln chewed the bite he'd taken of the bread and inhaled.

"I wasn't sure I wanted to see you again."

The statement cut deep even though it proved her instincts were correct. "Yet here we are."

He'd propped an arm up, his body turned toward her, and he lifted his glass. "Here we are. To fresh starts."

She clinked her glass with his. "To… romance resets," she whispered, quoting Izzy's comment from that fateful meeting with Marsali.

Lincoln's brown-eyed gaze sparkled in the light of the fire and held hers with an intensity that left her trembling from nerves and excitement and anticipation of whatever the future would hold.

"I did a lot of thinking after our first date, and it finally dawned on me that I owe you an apology, Amelia."

"For?"

"Scaring you away all those years ago. I knew what your life was like growing up and taking care of your siblings. Weight of the responsibilities you carried. And there I was asking you to trade one anchor for another. I didn't get it then, but now, as a dad and an adult, I see it clearly. I'm sorry."

She tightened her grip on the glass in her hand but lowered it to her lap, his words touching the deepest recesses of her soul. "It *was* a lot of pressure. My parents didn't want me to go away to college because it meant losing childcare. I constantly argued with them, and then you… More than anything, though, I'm sorry I wasn't there for you when you needed me to be. I hated myself for that but I just couldn't *stay*. It scared me so badly that if I married you I'd never be able to find out who I was supposed to be. The real me."

Lincoln leaned closer, his fingertips lightly brushing her hair away from her cheek. A moment passed. Two. Then he slid his hand to her nape and tugged her toward him, his lips covering hers in a bittersweet kiss that sealed the past in the past and freed the future to be whatever they made it.

By the time the kissing ended, they were both breathing heavily and leaning hard against one another.

"I guess that hasn't changed."

"Mmm. Nope," she said, her body practically buzzing. Desire had never been a problem for them. Ever. "But, um, maybe we should… slow things down a bit?" Had she really said that? Now? When her biological clock ticked away at light speed and slow was the last thing she needed? "At least until… we… um…"

While she tried to rein in her scrambled brain cells to form complete sentences, Lincoln grasped her trembling hand in his and lifted it to his lips to kiss, sucking the fruit juice from her fingertips one by one, his gaze holding hers. Yeah, like that didn't scramble the cells even more?

"Until we what, Amelia?"

Chapter 9

Lincoln wasn't sure what was going on in Amelia's beautiful head, but the sight of her, the taste of her had gone to his head faster than any drink. He'd watched her get out of her car and it was like nothing had changed. He saw her, wanted her, because in his mind, she had always been his.

Amelia was beautiful. Sexy and smart and down-to-earth. The kind of girl who didn't put on airs or pretend to be something she wasn't. But the girl he'd known had been replaced by an even sexier, more tantalizing version of the teenager who'd left Carolina Cove those twenty years ago. A woman more confident and aware of herself and her abilities—the person she'd needed to find within herself, like she'd said. The new Amelia drew him like a moth to flame.

Despite the mourning and love he felt and would always feel for Jill, in this moment, he experienced a nearly physical break of those ties. He'd loved his wife. Respected her. Cherished her until the day she'd died. But like Carter had said, the time had come, and the fact things had fallen into place as they had with Amelia… He wasn't a fool and he thanked God for the second chance.

"Um… until we get to know one another again. It's been a long time. We're not the same people we used to be," Amelia said in response to his question. "Attraction was never really a problem but… there's more t-to friendships than that."

Friendship. Was that what she wanted? It was a good place to start and he was okay with that. No one knew what the future held, after all, and the past had changed them both, as she'd said. But when he thought of the future… "As you wish."

She smiled at the phrase and his agreement. But the fact remained that a boat ride and firelight and the sweet taste of the fruit on her fingertips brought out his desire for more. For her and life and whatever came next. He'd force himself to move slowly. Somehow. Even though, more than anything, he wanted to sweep her up and claim her for all the world to see. Yes, they'd changed. And yet, they hadn't.

Lincoln exhaled and busied his hands by grabbing a piece of cheese from the plate between them. "Tell me more about you."

"What do you want to know?"

"Everything. I want to know everything, sweetheart."

They spent the next few hours quietly chatting about places they'd been, vacations they'd taken, celebrities she'd met while working on set and the idiosyncrasies she'd noticed about them. They shared life experiences that had forced them to change and grow as humans, and as evening changed to night, she leaned her head back to stare at the Milky Way above them. Lincoln used the opportunity to tug her closer and maneuver her so that her head was propped on a pillow in his lap. While she stared at the stars, he alternated between staring into the fire and at her, loving the way the light flickered over her delicate features.

He'd missed this. This… quiet peace and companionship that came with being with someone. Someone he cared for, someone familiar. Because as much as Amelia had changed, she was beautifully, intrinsically the same.

His watch dinged and he glanced at the face as a text came through.

"Everything okay?" Amelia asked.

"My son," Lincoln said. "He wants to know where I am. He's not used to his old man being out this late."

Amelia smiled at the statement and shifted, pushing herself upright on the packed sand bench. "I suppose it is getting late. We don't want the tide to change and get stuck."

He answered the text with a *be home in an hour or so* response even though he didn't want the night to end. Didn't want this to end. "What are you doing tomorrow? Are you free for lunch?"

She blinked at the questions, a smile curling the corners of her full lips up as she tilted her head to one side and stared at him.

"I'd like that very much."

They began gathering up everything and repacking the backpacks. Once that was done, Lincoln used the small bucket left there to dig out the space each time to douse the fire with sand. He refilled the bucket so it wouldn't blow away and left it in the pit for the next visit, knowing it wouldn't be far in the future.

Lincoln held Amelia's hand as they traipsed back toward the boat. He tossed the backpacks aboard first and then went back for Amelia. The moment he got close and swung her up against him, she pressed her mouth to his, giving him a slow, heady kiss that made him tighten his grip and hold her closer. The kiss ended way too soon for his liking.

"Thank you, Lincoln. Tonight was wonderful."

He hitched her a bit higher against his chest as he walked into the surf, welcoming the cold water since it cooled his jets and helped him regain some brain power. "You're very welcome."

Back on the *Pearl*, they weighed anchor and took their seats. He kept their speed low and slow, not wanting the night to end any sooner than it had to.

Back on solid ground with the boat safely moored at his slip, he tossed the backpacks into his SUV and held Amelia's hand as he walked her to her car. The marina was seemingly empty, no people to be heard or seen anywhere given the late hour.

Amelia unlocked her car, but before throwing her bag inside, she pulled a card from the folds and handed it to him.

"Since we've never officially done this—my numbers. So you don't have to go through Marsali."

He smiled and tucked the card into his shirt pocket since his shorts were still wet from the return wade to the boat. "I'll text you to make sure you make it home okay."

Silence descended between them, broken only by the

sounds of frogs and cicadas and the boats bobbing nearby.

Lincoln stepped close, bracing one palm on her car above her door. He lifted his other hand and brushed his knuckles over her cheek, leaning low to lightly rub his lips against hers. She parted instantly and he deepened the kiss, protecting her head with his forearm as he possessed her mouth with a kiss that demanded everything and wanted so much more.

Her hands gripped his chest, her nails lightly digging into his shirt and the muscle beneath. He groaned at the sensation and she gasped, dragging in a breath as he kissed his way along her jawline to her neck and the sensitive skin there.

He grazed her neck with his teeth and relished her moan in his ear, the shiver he felt run the length of her body. Lincoln shifted, raised his head, and kissed her again and again, but it wasn't enough to satisfy the craving growing inside of him.

"Might wanna take that somewhere private," a male voice called. "Never alone out here."

Lincoln felt Amelia freeze against him, the comment a dash of cold water they both needed. He turned and spied the man and his dog crossing the parking lot and entering the trail leading to the campgrounds nearby.

"Busted," Amelia said, her voice throaty and revealing her own need.

The awareness that she'd been just as caught up in the moment left his hands clenching. "Mm. I guess we were." He pressed a light, chaste kiss on her lips. "Go home, Amelia. Before I drag you into that backseat."

Amelia stared up at him and he wondered at her thoughts. Her gaze lowered to his mouth, and she raised herself on tiptoe, pressing several quick kisses to his lips before she dropped down onto the seat behind her.

He closed her safely inside and watched as she started the car and drove away, unlike their last date when she'd driven up to the restaurant and picked up the blond who'd sat at the bar while they had dinner. The sight had confused him at first, but then he praised Amelia's forethought, glad she wasn't taking chances when it came to meeting strangers, vetted or not.

The ride home was uncomfortable thanks to his wet clothing. He'd brought another change of clothes, but since he lived five minutes away and a shower beckoned, it seemed senseless. Especially when it meant more laundry.

Lincoln entered his house and was taking care of the leftover food and trash when Brendan walked into the room.

"Hey. Why are you wet?"

"Hey, yourself. I, uh, took the boat out and… had a date." Lincoln waited for Brendan to comment.

"Really?"

That was it? No drama? "Yeah."

"Cool. Did you have fun?"

It seemed weird to be having this conversation with his son but Lincoln nodded. "I did. We're going to lunch tomorrow for a third date."

"Third? You must like her."

A thought formed, and even though it didn't fall under the category of taking things slow as Amelia had suggested, he said, "I do. I'd like you and Breanne to meet Amelia before you leave for college. Especially since you won't be back until Thanksgiving."

"Okay. Whatever."

"You're… okay with this?"

Brendan shrugged. "Yeah. I mean, she must be nice if you want us to meet her."

"She is. We're just friends but… I'm looking forward to spending more time with her. Amelia and I… We dated in high school. Before I met your mom."

Brendan was quiet a long moment, and Lincoln kept working the cleanup while keeping an eye on his son's changing expressions.

"Mom wouldn't want you to be alone, Dad. Especially when Bree and I will be gone soon. I'm glad you're doing this. Hey, is that that cheese I like?"

Brendan had a bottomless pit for a stomach, but Lincoln chuckled at the swift change in topic. "Have at it. All yours. Where's your sister?"

"Been in her room all night. I tried to get her to go out with me and the gang but she didn't want to. She might be sick. I heard her hurling in the bathroom this morning."

Lincoln stilled at the news. "Did you check on her when you got back?"

"Yeah. She was asleep."

"Clean up when you're finished. I'm going to go check on her." Lincoln left the kitchen and jogged up the stairs. He quietly opened Breanne's door and found her snuggled under her covers, her blond hair shining brightly in the light beaming in from behind him. Maybe it was just a bug. Or nerves over leaving for school? She'd always had a nervous stomach. He'd talk to her about it in the morning.

Lincoln went to his bedroom and stripped out of the wet clothes to shower but texted Amelia's number as he'd promised.

Home safe and sound, she texted back. *Thanks again. I had fun tonight.*

I'm glad. I want you to meet my kids tomorrow. Okay?

The three little dots appeared on the screen but then disappeared again. No response. He waited a few more seconds before adding, *I know it might be rushing things, Amelia, but they're leaving for college soon. Say yes. How about a coffee date with the kids before our lunch? London's Lattes. Eleven a.m.?*

Once again, a pause. Then the three little dots reappeared.

I'll be there. Good night, Lincoln. Sweet dreams.

Sweet dreams. It's what she'd tell him on the phone every night when they'd dated. The memory brought a smile to his lips as he moved into the bathroom and turned on the shower.

Amelia was fun. Always up for a good time. She smiled a lot. Laughed. Pulled him in with her beautiful eyes and made him feel like a man. She loved to travel. Her past was proof of that. The kids would be away at college in a matter of weeks. Plenty of time for him to plan a trip. Maybe when she finished her current project they could go somewhere? Do some of the things they'd talked about, dreamed about doing, before life had changed their plans?

Chapter 10

The following morning, Amelia took a deep breath that failed to steady the nerves attacking her at the thought of meeting Lincoln's children so soon. At eighteen, they were hardly kids, but they weren't exactly adults either. More than that, they'd lost their mother and Lincoln was just starting to date. How would they take his bringing them to meet her?

She inhaled once more and slowly released it on a five count. Nope. Didn't work that time either. Maybe… Maybe she should cancel? Force Lincoln to wait at least a bit longer?

"Hey. Have you been here long?" Lincoln asked.

Amelia opened her eyes—when had she closed them?—and found Lincoln looking every bit as nervous as she was. Behind him stood a lankier, younger version of him she recognized with a blink. "Wow."

Her comment brought out Lincoln's lazy grin. "Yeah. Spittin' image and all that."

Brendan was indeed his father's mirror image at that

age. The younger version was curious about her, too, and she forced a smile when he continued to stare.

"Amelia, my son and daughter, Brendan and Breanne. Guys, this is Amelia."

Pleasantries were exchanged, and while Breanne said the proper words without a hint of animosity, it was obvious she'd like to be anywhere but there. After the introductions, the trio moved to the counter to place their orders, and after paying, Lincoln left the kids there to wait on their drinks.

Lincoln approached her at the table and took the chair beside her.

"Hey. You okay?"

"You made very handsome and beautiful children," she said, a niggle of jealousy entering her tone even though she knew she was the very reason those kids weren't hers and Lincoln's.

Lincoln must have caught on to her thoughts because he frowned.

"Amelia?"

"I'm fine. Nerves," she said, shaking her head and pasting on a smile. "Sorry."

The twins approached with cups and plates, and Brendan went back to retrieve another two plates and set them in front of Amelia and Lincoln.

"Sometimes you need to eat dessert first," Lincoln murmured, scooting the chocolate cake toward her.

The next hour was spent chatting about colleges and dorms, with Lincoln being the dad she always knew he would be because he went into lecture mode a time or two, much to the kids' rolled-eyed upset. Amelia tried to keep the conversation flowing by asking the kids questions so they'd talk about themselves and their activities, but Brendan seemed to be the more talkative of the two.

"Dad said you dated when you were our age," Brendan said. "Why'd you break up?"

Amelia noted that the statement drew Breanne's attention, and the girl shifted her focus from her plate to Amelia. "Uh, well, I was eighteen, fresh out of high school, and I had big dreams."

"And I was eighteen, had just become guardian to your uncle, and wanted to settle down."

"The timing just wasn't right," Amelia added.

"Good thing, too, or neither of you would be here," Lincoln said with a pointed look.

"I miss Mom," Breanne murmured. The girl's eyes widened and she sat back in her chair. "I'm sorry. I didn't mean it like that... I just meant..."

"It's okay," Amelia said before Lincoln could say anything. Given the flash of upset on his face, Amelia tried to stop a scolding before it began. "Of course you miss your mom. You have some big changes coming up in the next few weeks, and I'm sure she would've loved to have been here for them. To help you."

Brendan glanced at his watch and pushed his plate away.

"I'm supposed to meet the guys on the pier to fish. Bree, you coming or not?" Brendan asked. "Jax'll be there."

Amelia watched as the girl struggled to decide, every thought racing across her face and marring her beautiful features.

"You don't have to go, sweetheart," Lincoln said. "Jaxon and Bree broke up not long ago," Lincoln informed Amelia.

"I'm sorry to hear that," Amelia said to the girl, her heart tugging because of the emotion so readily apparent on Breanne's face. "You're welcome to keep us company."

"No. Thanks, though. It was nice meeting you," the girl said to Amelia.

"You, too. It was lovely to meet you both," Amelia said.

Lincoln told the kids to be careful, and Amelia watched as the twins left the coffee shop. Lincoln had said once that they were similar in looks but different in personality, and she could certainly see that was the case. Brendan was his father made over, while his sister was a mixture of Lincoln and, Amelia guessed, Breanne's mother.

"Okay, fess up. What was that look about earlier? The statement about the twins when we first got here?"

Oh, when would she ever learn to keep her mouth shut? "You caught me."

"I did. Now what was it?"

"Honestly?"

"Always."

"It was a moment of regret."

"Regret?"

She struggled to maintain eye contact and, in the end, had to look away. "That they weren't mine, Lincoln. I looked up and this gorgeous man and his beautiful children walked in and all I could do was sit here and think, *What if I hadn't...* It got me, you know? That was the look. Regret and... the shoulda, woulda, couldas—even though we both know it probably would've been a disaster."

She braved a look at Lincoln and caught the shock

rolling over his face before he smoothed his wrinkled forehead and used his fork to poke at the cake remaining on his plate.

Amelia watched as he set the fork down and turned toward her, braced his arm on the back of her chair.

"What about now?" he asked. "We've had a few dates. Shared a few kisses. You've met my kids. The past is the past, but what happens now?"

She knew why he asked the question. Why he demanded an answer from her. He'd put himself out there once. Asked her, *begged* her to marry him. She'd hurt him in the worst way and now he was wary. Even though this was only their third date, she had a feeling Lincoln was as drawn to her as she was to him, but he was afraid of getting too close.

Amelia lifted her hand and lightly touched his cheek, loving the way the stubble felt beneath her fingertips. "I think… I'd like to know what I've missed out on all of these years. You?"

His gaze searched hers.

"I think I'd like that, too."

She watched how his gaze lowered to her mouth and held, the visual caress every bit as tantalizing as the kisses he'd mentioned.

Amelia bit her lip and dared ask the question in the back of her mind. "Um, I suppose I should tell Marsali not to fix me up anymore?"

He turned his face into her fingers and kissed them, his gaze back on hers.

"You should. I plan to do the same."

Amelia felt the sting of tears but blinked hard, blaming stress and her upcoming cycle for the sudden rush in response to his words, in addition to the stress of the film schedule on her calendar. "Then I guess that's what comes next."

Time. She needed more time before they broached the subject of whatever came after *this*. She wanted to now but there was a process. A protocol? The words were there on the tip of her tongue but how would he react? Dating, engagement, marriage, babies. That was the order of things. Because asking a man to father a child on their third date wasn't exactly covered in social skills, and they couldn't rush something so precious.

But she also couldn't help but wonder—when would be a good time to ask?

Chapter 11

Lincoln knocked on Amelia's condo door the following Friday and waited for her to answer. They'd both had extremely busy work weeks, which meant communication had been done through calls, texts, and a few video chats. Finally the weekend approached and a scheduling change freed her up for an evening out.

"Coming!"

He smiled at her response and looked around the hallway. The area where she lived seemed as safe as any other, but he didn't like the fact the elevators and stairs weren't keyed with a security code.

The door opened and Amelia stepped back to invite him in with a smile. She wore a black dress that bared her shoulders and ended mid-thigh. She'd pulled her hair half up with tendrils left loose and wore heels that added length to her long legs. He suppressed a low growl of appreciation and silently thanked Marsali for matching them up.

"Sunflowers. They're beautiful, Lincoln, thank you."

He handed over the bouquet, but when she turned away, he quickly caught her arm and tugged her close, bent, and stole a kiss from her lips. She tasted minty and warm, and his pulse picked up speed. "You're welcome," he said against her lips. "You look stunning, Amelia."

He liked that his compliment and kiss left her rosy-cheeked and dreamy-eyed. Things like that did a lot for a man's ego, and after being a widower and a boring dad, the boost it gave him went a long way.

"You're looking pretty handsome yourself. Um, make yourself at home while I put these in water."

Lincoln perused her condo while she moved toward the kitchen. The open floor plan and high ceilings made for a nice space with the kitchen, dining, and living area one large room. Patio doors opened to a screened porch with a river view.

She definitely had a designer's touch. Her home was warm and inviting, a mix of blues and grays and some light tans that made him think of the varying shades of sky, ocean, and sand without being gimmicky with beach themes so popular in homes along the coast. "This is nice. You did a great job decorating. I might have to have you help stage some of my listings."

"Thank you. I like it. Easy maintenance, easy to clean, and close to downtown so I don't have to deal with traffic, especially for those early-morning shooting schedules when simply rolling out of bed is hard. It works for me."

"How many bedrooms?" He asked because of his profession, but given the color that filled Amelia's cheeks, Lincoln could tell the query took her mind to other places. Places they'd been twenty years ago. His immediately followed and he inhaled in a poor attempt to clear his mind of the temptation she posed and the self-imposed rule of taking things slow.

"Two. Enough room to have the out-of-town siblings visit one at a time but not for the whole crew to descend at once since my mom and dad downsized and there aren't enough bedrooms to stay there. Okay," she said, arranging the flowers. "Done."

She crossed into the living area and set the vase on the coffee table. Lincoln tried and failed to keep his eyes on her face and not on her behind and the length of leg revealed as she bent and her skirt inched higher.

She straightened abruptly and caught him looking, and once again a pretty flush of color filled her cheeks.

"Um… I just need to grab my bag and I'm ready."

He nodded, not going to deny or excuse the desire for her that he knew she'd seen on his features. He couldn't help it. Maybe it was because of their previous relationship, but he knew that wasn't entirely the reason. Amelia was more fascinating now as a grown woman, more intriguing, more beautiful. More everything.

Amelia moved toward a chair near the door and plucked a sparkling purse from the seat.

"So, where are we going?"

Drawn back to their plans for the evening, he slowly moved toward her and took her soft hand in his. "You'll see."

He led the way to the door, waiting patiently while she locked up behind them.

Lincoln drove them to a rooftop restaurant not far from where she lived. The restaurant overlooked the downtown area and riverfront, and the views were spec-tacular.

A guitarist played on the far side of the rooftop, and after placing their dinner order, they chatted about their respective weeks for a few minutes before Lincoln snagged her hand and pulled her onto the makeshift dance floor.

Back in the day, they danced like the awkward teenagers they'd been, her arms around his neck, his at her waist. Now he held her hand tucked close to his chest, lips at her temple as they swayed in time to the music like the couples did in old black-and-white movies.

"Did you ever think, twenty years later, we'd be here? Like this?"

Amelia tilted her head back and stared up at him, and Lincoln found himself lost in the depths of her soft green gaze as she waited for him to answer. "No," he said softly, his voice emerging gruff. "But now I can't imagine being anywhere else."

JUST WHEN SHE thought Lincoln couldn't do anything sweeter, say anything to make her want him more… he did. And the last of Amelia's reservations about whether or not he was ready for a relationship after the death of his wife fizzled in that very moment.

It also cemented the fact that she needed to talk to Lincoln. Really talk to him. Open up and tell him what she wanted more than anything.

Hopefully he'd be on board, but what if he wasn't? What then? Could she give up her dream of being a mother? Would she be okay with letting go of that dream if the alternative meant losing Lincoln?

It was crazy how quickly things had progressed between them, feelings and emotions buried for so long resurfacing faster and stronger than ever. The texts and calls and video chats had revealed more of their grown-up lives and had cranked up the level of intimacy since a few of those times they'd been sleepy-eyed in bed just talking about their days and more honest than they would've been fully awake and on guard. But all of those talks had been real and heartfelt.

Amelia tucked her head back into place beneath his chin and closed her eyes, reveling in the moment. The breeze blew the curls she'd left hanging, and they tickled her neck and added to the sensation of being held. His cologne teased her nose, a heart-squeezing mix of her favorites, sandalwood and spice. In Lincoln's arms, the world faded away until it was just the two of them, alone on a rooftop beneath the stars, swaying their way through the next couple of songs before heading back to their seat when their waitress gained Lincoln's attention and told him their food had arrived.

They settled in with their dinner and laughed and teased and shared favorites, feeding one another like couples sometimes do. Amelia had just finished when she heard someone call Lincoln's name.

"Hayes, is that you?" a man asked.

Amelia watched as a man and woman approached them and Lincoln quickly wiped his mouth and stood.

"John, Priscilla, it's good to see you."

"And you. Who's this?" John asked, smiling at Amelia.

"My apologies," Lincoln said, performing the introductions.

When Priscilla shifted uncomfortably on her feet and rubbed a hand over her very pregnant belly, Amelia asked if they wanted to join them so she could get off her feet.

"Of course," Lincoln said, his hand sweeping out in welcome. "Forgive my manners. Please, join us."

"Oh, thank you," Priscilla said once she scooted in by Amelia. "We've been standing at the bar for a while, waiting on a table. You're so sweet to let us intrude on your dinner."

"You're fine," Amelia said to her.

"Have you and Lincoln been together long?" Priscilla asked.

Amelia glanced at Lincoln and found his gaze suddenly focused on the interior of the restaurant. The restaurant was crowded, but she knew Lincoln had heard the woman's question. Was Lincoln uncomfortable being seen out on a date? She supposed for a widower of several years, it would be an adjustment. "Um, no, not long. When are you due?" Amelia asked the younger woman, guessing her to be in her mid to late twenties.

"Not for another month," Priscilla said. "Never again will I be pregnant *in* the summer *in* the south. Not if I can help it."

"I'm sure the heat makes it difficult," Amelia said.

"I've been living in the pool just to keep cool and attempt to stay in shape. This is our second. It's another boy, so we hope the next one will be a girl."

"Hey, now. One at a time there, sweetheart," John said, eavesdropping on their conversation.

Amelia turned to study Priscilla's husband and guessed John to be her and Lincoln's age. It struck her how different the two men were. Lincoln with his grown kids and about to have an empty nest while John and his young wife were just starting and apparently not finished yet.

Where would Lincoln fall when she finally worked up the courage to broach the subject of children?

Unease settled deep within her. She couldn't continue to put off this conversation. At the same time, though, she didn't want to ruin things between them when they were going so well.

"She hasn't had this one and she's working on the next. Babe, just ask Lincoln here why God gives parents teenagers," John said to his wife. "You might not be in such a hurry then."

Priscilla looked at Lincoln with an inquiring smile.

"It was a bad day several years ago," Lincoln stated. "I didn't mean it, but John has never let me live it down."

"But he said," John continued, seemingly determined to tell the story since Lincoln wasn't, "that God gave parents teenagers so they wouldn't mind it when they left home. We'll have two teenagers and you're already wanting to add a third? Lincoln is over here counting down the days until his kids go off to college. Where was it you want to go again? Scotland? Or did you switch back to New Zealand?"

"I haven't decided," Lincoln said.

"But he's ready to travel and have some fun," John added.

"Yeah, well, whatever." Priscilla laughed and shrugged. "I'm not the only one wanting a girl. You know good and well you want a baby girl you can spoil rotten. And I'm sure Lincoln was looking into those trips because he's going to miss his kids when they're gone. Right, Lincoln?"

Lincoln smiled and winked at Priscilla but didn't give a definitive answer, Amelia noted, her heart sinking at the awareness.

"We're just teasing you, honey."

"I know. Just like I know we'll keep trying for a girl," Priscilla said pointedly. "Every mother should have the chance to buy the frilly little dresses and bows and shoes." To Amelia, Priscilla said, "Trust me, our house needs more estrogen to even out the testosterone."

"You had the right idea," John said to Lincoln. "Twins on the first try. One of each, and boom—done. You're going to be sitting on a beach somewhere enjoying life while I'm still changing dirty diapers."

"You'll get there eventually," Lincoln said. "It happens before you know it."

Amelia listened and watched Lincoln's responses to the conversation until the men began discussing real estate. Priscilla murmured an apology when she had to answer a text from their babysitter, and Amelia found herself sitting there silently, wondering how it was possible to want both worlds. She'd love to explore the world with Lincoln at her side, but she'd also love a home full of giggles and little-boy engine sounds.

The restaurant noises faded away as Amelia retreated into her thoughts even more. Her appointment at the clinic was coming up fast, every day that passed disappearing more rapidly than the one before it. She had to make a decision, but to do that, she needed to know where Lincoln stood on the matter of parenthood.

Know where they stood as a couple. Would they see eye to eye about starting a family? Or was Lincoln "one and done" because he and his first wife had the twins?

Given the conversation that had just taken place, did she already know the answer?

Chapter 12

"Play your cards right and he'd agree to just about anything right now," Carter said from somewhere nearby.

His son's laughter followed the statement and pulled Lincoln from his dazed state. He focused on his son and brother. "I was listening."

"Uh-huh," Brendan said, grinning.

"Look, here's a bit of advice. If your uncle suggests it, I don't recommend trying it," Lincoln said to Brendan. "And you," he said to Carter, "need to remember Piper will be around at least another fourteen years for me to pay you back for whatever you're trying to instigate."

Carter chuckled at the warning and flipped the burgers on the grill. "So you going to tell us how things are going with Amelia?"

"No." Because how could he after last night's strange ending? Their date had started off fine. Drinks, dancing, dinner. They'd laughed and talked and done more than a little contact flirting, with brushes of fingertips and light, stroking hands that couldn't linger due to their public presence but got the point across. Until—

"Come on, Dad. She seemed nice enough or you wouldn't have introduced her to me and Bree."

"Agreed," Carter stated in a low voice. "Because most guys would keep the hotties away from the kids for the first few months at least."

Maybe he should've. After last night's quick exit into her condo, Lincoln wondered if maybe he'd rushed things. Rushed Amelia. Because why else would she go from warm and welcoming to silent and distant so quickly? Had he said something he shouldn't? He tried to review the various conversations in his mind and all had seemed good until Priscilla and John had joined them at their table.

He'd been uncomfortable at first, knowing John wouldn't keep Lincoln's dating status to himself but would share with the others in his real estate company. The last thing Lincoln needed was his employees and colleagues focused on his love life rather than their jobs. Had Amelia sensed his unease and taken it to mean something else?

Time had flown since he'd introduced Amelia to the twins, and even though it didn't seem possible, the twins would be leaving for school in a matter of days. He'd rented a cargo van to haul their stuff north and help them settle in and hoped he didn't make a fool of himself when he had to leave them there.

He'd heard little from Amelia since their date because Amelia was required on set during filming.

"There he goes again. Dad, you've got it bad," Brendan said.

Lincoln inhaled and resigned himself to an interrogation. He just wished he had more answers. "Should we call Breanne down from her room to hear this so I don't have to repeat myself about how much I enjoy Amelia's company?"

"She's gone." Brendan grabbed a soda from the cooler and popped the top. "She left an hour or so ago. I thought you knew."

He hadn't. And seeing as how this was supposed to be a family dinner… "Any idea where she went?"

"No. Maybe Jo's house. Or Kari's. Bree's been acting weird lately."

Lincoln exchanged a glance with Carter, and the two of them turned in unison to face Brendan. "Weird how?" Lincoln said. "Is she worried about going away to school?"

"The breakup with Jax?" Carter asked.

"I don't know. I guess. The whole breakup thing is definitely part of it. She and Jax talked a little at the pier a few weeks ago when we fished, but she didn't seem any better afterwards."

"Daddy, look," Piper said from her kids' table.

His niece lifted the picture she'd drawn.

"Is that us?" Carter asked.

"Uh-huh. All of us. And the lady you said Uncle Linc is dating. They're gonna get married."

Carter started chuckling while Brendan looked at the drawing and pointed at Lincoln.

"Is that why my dad has hearts for eyes?"

Lincoln cleared his throat. "Don't rush things, sweetheart. We're dating. Friends. That's all. I only introduced her to my kids because they're leaving for college and I wanted them to meet before they left."

The words seemed to satisfy Brendan, and his son asked Piper why his feet were so big.

Brendan moved to the table and folded his long legs down to sit on one of the tiny chairs, and Lincoln snuck a photo of them. Bren resembled a praying mantis folded up as he was, but the image of the cousins was too sweet to pass up as Brendan grabbed a sheet of paper and began his own drawing.

"Want me to talk to Bree?" Carter asked in a low voice meant not to carry. "Might be easier to talk to someone who isn't her old man."

Lincoln shoved himself to his feet to go inside to get the burger fixings and check on the sweet potato fries in the oven. "We'll both give it a try. Hopefully she'll talk to one of us. Keep an eye on the kids after dinner, though, would you? Amelia said she had to work late and was going to stop and get some groceries on her way home. I want to surprise her and at least walk her to the door before she collapses from exhaustion."

"That bad, huh?" Carter asked.

"I never knew filming could be so rough. She's starting to get shadows under her eyes from the stress of getting it all prepped for today. She says it's normal due to the schedule, but I feel like there's something else bothering her."

"And you think showing up at her house after a long day will help?"

"I just want to see her. Kiss her good-night and see if she'll talk to me."

Carter shook his head and released a low whistle.

"Man, you do have it bad."

• • •

AMELIA PARKED outside the store on the way home and walked inside. Filming weeks were always difficult, but the last couple had been especially exhausting as the set-prep took some unusual turns.

Normally she was better prepared for filming to begin with groceries stocked and all the essentials in place, but her focus had been so skewed because of dating Lincoln that she'd neglected to do any of it. And since she hated going to the big-box stores, the pharmacy closest to her condo would have to do for now.

She grabbed a cart and went to the makeup aisle first for mascara since she'd dropped her wand in the toilet this morning while trying to blacken her lashes. Thankfully she'd had a backup in her beach bag to finish the job. She definitely liked being prepared, because she never knew when her schedule might change, so she tried to keep two of everything when possible, especially things like grooming essentials.

Shampoo and conditioner were next, along with new razors. She checked the Post-it note of scribbled items written during her break earlier on set and headed toward food. A couple cans of soup, an emergency bag of Milanos, some juice, and much-needed coffee. And wine. She couldn't forget the wine.

Amelia hurried through the aisles, eager to get home and out of her uncomfortable clothes to crash on her couch with a rerun of *Friends* and a chocolate bar. Maybe Lincoln would call. Maybe she would call him? She'd been hesitant to initiate contact today, mostly because she had yet to work up the courage to speak honestly about her desire for kids. How did you broach something like that?

Her thoughts crashed like a wave against the sand

when she spotted Breanne standing at the far end of the aisle staring wide-eyed at the… birth control?

Oh, no.

Amelia froze even though her mind went crazy with potential disasters. She desperately wanted to turn the cart around and head the other way, but she needed a package of crackers to go with the soup, and those were at the end of her current aisle. *Closer to Breanne.*

Amelia tucked her chin to her chest and had just snagged the cracker box and was ready to make her sharp right turn for a clean getaway when she heard Breanne gasp.

"Am-melia. Hi. Um…"

Amelia held up a hand before the girl could go any further. "Hi. Yeah. I'm not sure what the protocol is for this situation given where you're standing so… I'm going to go with stay safe and… goodbye."

Amelia took a step, pushing the cart, when she heard Breanne's bitter response.

"Too late for that now."

Amelia stopped, shock rolling through her and gathering speed like an avalanche. She couldn't just leave after *that* statement, could she? "Breanne…?"

The girl burst into tears there in the store, and Amelia gaped, unsure of what to do. A second passed before she put her feet in motion and left the cart in the break between the aisles, rushing toward the girl and enveloping Lincoln's daughter in her arms. "Shh. Shhhh. Hey. It's okay. It'll be okay."

"It won't," the girl sobbed against Amelia's shoulder. "What if I am? I left the island and drove all the way here so no one would see me and now *you're* here and what am I going to do when I tell my dad and he *explodes* and school is starting and my life is *over* because I was stupid enough to think Jaxon loved me and wouldn't leave me?"

That was one long sentence in one equally long gush of breath. Amelia realized then that the birth control was positioned directly beside the pregnancy tests and that was what Breanne had been staring at with such panic. Amelia squeezed the girl tight again before she purposely but gently pushed her away. "Okay. Hey, look at me. Here's the plan. You are going to take my keys and go wait in my car. I'm the black Mercedes parked beside the handicapped spot as soon as you walk out the door. On the left. Okay? While you do that, I am going to buy a test for you along with my groceries. Then we'll… go back to my place and you'll have some privacy and an answer. One way or another. But you won't be alone. Okay?"

Lincoln's beautiful daughter blinked at her, silent tears still streaming down her face.

"Why are you helping me?"

Amelia tilted her head to one side and brushed the girl's tear-sodden hair away from her face. "Because if I'm ever blessed with a daughter and she needs help, I hope someone would step up for her. Right now? It's my turn to do this for you. Now get going. I'll be right there."

Breanne wiped her eyes, accepted Amelia's key fob. Amelia watched Breanne simply stand there, frozen by her fear.

"God, what am I going to do?" Breanne breathed softly, head down as she turned and walked away.

Amelia grabbed the pregnancy test on her trek toward the front of the store. She quickly pondered what Lincoln had told her about his twins and what she'd gleaned from their coffee date with them, remembering Breanne had mentioned her like of dark chocolate. This kind of situation called for emergency chocolate on a grand scale, so she grabbed several bars on her approach to the checkout along with a miniature dog stuffie that was cute and just seemed like the thing to get to help with a bad day.

Minutes later, she and Breanne were on their way toward her condo.

"What about my car?"

"I'll drive you back later," Amelia said.

"Dad said you're working a lot. I'm sorry to be so much trouble."

"It's no trouble," she said, even as her body dragged with fatigue and the need for sleep, the restful kind that came on rainy days when she had nowhere to be and could lie in bed dozing for hours past her wake-up time.

"So you want kids?"

Amelia stopped at a red light, her grip tight on the steering wheel. "What?"

"You said if you ever had a daughter… back in the store."

"Oh. Yeah, I do, actually. Very badly."

"Does that mean you want kids with my dad?"

Oh, that made for one touchy subject. "I… don't know yet. We haven't reached that stage in our relationship, but it's important to me, so I suppose it's something we need to discuss very soon due to my… age."

"You're almost forty, like Dad, right?"

Amelia nodded and tried not to cringe. "Yup. It's not uncommon for women my age to get pregnant, but it can be more difficult, especially if there are issues. I have endometriosis. Have you heard of that?"

"I remember that from biology class. It's gunk that keeps you from getting pregnant, right?"

"Right. So even though I want to get pregnant, it might not happen for me." Regardless of whether it was with Lincoln… or a sperm-bank baby as Izzy liked to say.

"Yeah, well, if I am, I'll trade you," Breanne muttered.

The car behind her honked when Amelia missed the light turning green, and she stepped on the gas. "Children are blessings, Breanne. I know you're scared and hurting right now, but I don't believe any child is a mistake. Ever."

The girl went quiet at Amelia's statement, and she wondered if she'd said too much.

"I heard Uncle Carter teasing Dad about hiring a matchmaker. Did you hire her hoping you'd meet someone and get pregnant?"

Amelia had to remind herself of two things: Breanne was Lincoln's child and concerned about her father… and she was an eighteen-year-old woman facing the future with potential pregnancy hormones. "I… didn't hire Marsali, actually. My friend did."

"Because?"

"Breanne, I'm not sure we should be discussing—"

"I'm about to pee on a stick with you outside the door. I think we can pretty much discuss anything at this point."

True. Definitely true. "Fine. I'm serious about having a baby, so I was researching alternative ways of making it happen. Izzy—my best friend—thinks I shouldn't give up on romance and finding someone, so *she* hired Marsali, and your father and I met."

"That is seriously cool."

"You think?"

"Yeah. But if you're okay with being with Dad now, why did you break up in high school?"

Another red light. Great. More time to get grilled by the teenager. "It's complicated."

"More complicated than getting knocked up at eighteen even though you used protection but it broke?"

A huff of a laugh left her chest. "Okay, you win. Back then, your father asked me to marry him because he wanted to settle down and make a home for Carter. I wasn't ready. I wanted to travel and go to college— Hey, you wanted to know," she said when the girl flinched. "I know it's tricky to think about right now, but just hang tight until you take that test and have a definitive answer, okay?"

Breanne nodded and Amelia got the car moving again when the light changed.

"Does my dad want more kids?" Breanne asked.

Amelia inhaled. "I honestly don't know. That's something we have yet to discuss but I hope so. Would that bother you?" She made the turn into her condo complex along the river.

"I don't know. Maybe. Especially if I'm… Oh, no. No, no, no, this can't be happening."

"What?" Amelia asked, slowing the vehicle to glance at Breanne. "What is it?"

"Is that my *Dad*?"

Chapter 13

Lincoln blinked at the sight of Breanne sitting beside Amelia in her SUV. He waited for them to park in Amelia's appointed spot and stood from the bench where he'd sat waiting. "Hey. What's going on here?"

Amelia looked a little wide-eyed and flushed, but it was nothing compared to Breanne's pale-as-death complexion.

"I, um, saw Breanne in a store and she was upset over her breakup, so I offered some company and chocolate therapy," Amelia told him, tilting her head to the side to give him better access to the cheek she offered.

"Is that really it?" he murmured as he brushed his lips over her face.

"Of course. What are you doing here?"

"You said you were working late and stopping by the store, so I thought I'd come help carry in your groceries and kiss you good-night."

"Lincoln... that's sweet."

Lincoln greeted his quiet daughter as he opened the rear access to gather the plastic bags.

"Oh, we can get those," Amelia said.

"Yeah. I'll do it, Dad. G-go with Amelia."

He gathered up the bags in one hand and pressed the button to close the door with his free hand. "I've got them. Let's go have some chocolate," he said, inviting himself along in the hopes that Breanne might open up a bit more about what was going on with her with Amelia around.

The ladies exchanged a long look Lincoln couldn't interpret, but Amelia turned and urged Breanne toward the walkway leading to the elevator. The ride up was suspiciously silent and Lincoln's unease grew. "You two seem… distracted."

"We're fine," they said in unison.

Okay. Nothing strange about that, he mused.

The elevator door opened and Breanne bolted out of the enclosure. Amelia led the way to her door and unlocked it with hands that trembled slightly.

Lincoln carried the bags into the kitchen.

"I'm going out on the balcony. Okay?" Breanne asked, sounding urgent and looking a little pale.

"Sure," Amelia said. "Lincoln, thank you. I'll put everything away later. There's nothing perishable. Just leave it."

"Okay. But we can't forget the chocolate," he said, opening the bag most likely to contain it. His lungs seized at what he found inside, and he couldn't get air in or out.

Amelia's body suddenly slammed against his chest, trapping his arm between them. She pressed her hand over his mouth, hard.

"Take a breath and don't say a word until you can do so without yelling."

His gaze locked on hers and his nostrils flared as he inhaled. After a long moment, she slowly removed her hand but didn't move away. He swallowed hard and cleared his throat. "As much as I can't stand the thought of you with another man, please tell me this test is for you," he begged, his voice emerging husky and low.

"I wish it was but no," she said. "It's not."

The ground under his feet shifted, and he found himself shoved backward into a hastily pulled out chair. Breanne was— Amelia wanted— "You want *kids*?"

Amelia blinked at him, her expression one of hurt and disappointment.

"This is not the time for that discussion, but yes, I do. Now, Breanne is going to come out of that bathroom soon, and when she does, you need to be ready."

"How did this… I'm going to kill him."

"No, you're not. They used protection. It didn't work," she informed him.

Yeah, that was way more information than he ever wanted to know about his daughter's sex life.

"I found her sobbing in the middle of a store because she's terrified her life is over. Lincoln? *Lincoln.*"

"What?"

"You have to be here for Breanne no matter how much you want to shout at the world right now. Okay?"

He wiped a shaking hand over his face and stared up at her, trying to process her words and make them make sense. "You can't want kids, Amelia. This is what they do to you. They make you fall in love with them, and then they grow up and rip your heart out." He pressed a hand to his chest and rubbed the tightness there. "I think I'm having a heart attack."

Standing beside the chair, Amelia wrapped her arms around him with a soft laugh and cradled his head against her. He felt her kiss his head, and he nuzzled against the softness she offered, well aware of the way she shivered at his touch.

"I think you're having an anxiety attack. Breathe, Lincoln. It'll be okay, because whether she is or isn't, you love her. Right?"

He wrapped his arms around her frame and squeezed, wishing he could dive into her warmth and love and not surface for days, weeks. He had to talk to Amelia about her thoughts on children, but she was right about one thing—now wasn't the time.

"Dad?"

Lincoln opened his eyes to find Breanne standing six feet away eyeing him like a cobra about to strike. "Hey, kiddo."

Breanne's gaze shifted to the test lying out in the open on the counter.

"Daddy, I'm sorry," she said, unable to make eye contact.

Lincoln released Amelia and stood, up and out of the chair in a second flat. He drew Breanne into his arms and held her while she cried, head buried in his chest like she had her whole life. "I know. It'll be okay. How about we take that test and know for sure, eh?"

Amelia grabbed the box from atop the bag and held it out to Breanne.

"You know what to do?"

Bree nodded.

"I bought a twin pack, so if you don't believe it the

first time, you can do it again. Or take them both at the same time to compare."

"Thanks, Amelia," Bree said.

"You're welcome. Go. I'll distract your dad."

Breanne took the box and avoided eye contact as she left the room once more. Lincoln turned toward Amelia and saw her unloading the rest of the groceries. "You… Thank you. For helping her. Me."

"You're welcome."

"You look tired. Have you eaten today?"

"Not much. But I'm not hungry now."

A huff left him and he raked his fingers through his short hair. "Yeah, me either." He closed the distance between them and pulled Amelia into his arms, lowered his head for a kiss that pressed lips and foreheads together and simply held, unmoving, for a time. It wasn't a sexual type of kiss but an appreciative one, bonding them together as they leaned against each other for strength. "You are amazing," he whispered. "I can't believe you brought her home with you."

"I couldn't exactly leave her there," she said, nuzzling the words against his mouth. "And you're not so bad yourself."

Lincoln gave her a real kiss before lifting his head to stare into her beautiful eyes. "You weren't serious about wanting kids, right? That was… I don't know, a joke?"

"Um… no?"

"No, what?"

"It wasn't a joke. Lincoln, I want to be a mother. And seeing as how I've waited so long, the sooner it happens the better."

He pulled away from her, shaken to his core once more by the earth-shattering revelation. "Amelia, I'm about to have an empty nest for the first time in my life. I became a guardian at *eighteen*… and I may be finding out I'm going to be a *grand*father in a matter of minutes. You expect me to want to add a kid to that?"

A noise alerted them to Bree's return. Lincoln took one look at his daughter's face and felt like he'd been sucker-punched. "Bree?"

Breanne cried as she ran toward him.

"I'm not! It's negative! They were both negative! I'm *not*!"

Lincoln lifted Breanne off her feet to hug her tight and swing her around, sharing her relief—until his gaze met Amelia's and he knew something bigger had just happened tonight as a result of the pregnancy scare.

He kissed Bree's cheek and lowered her to her feet.

"I'm glad you got the answer you wanted, Breanne," Amelia said softly. "Now I hope you don't mind, but I've had a really long day and I'm tired. All of the excitement has left me exhausted. Maybe you and your dad should go out somewhere to celebrate your news and talk privately?"

"Yeah. Okay," Breanne said as she walked over and hugged Amelia. "Thank you for everything. I'm so glad I saw you in the store, Amelia. You're the best. Thank you so much."

Lincoln watched as Amelia squeezed his daughter with the loving care of a woman who wanted to be a mother, and it cut him to the core. Their gazes locked once more, and his gut tightened when he saw her eyes fill with unshed tears.

"Me, too."

"Bree, give us a minute, okay?"

"Is everything all right?" Breanne asked, her head swiveling between the two of them.

Amelia cleared her throat and grabbed a chocolate bar from the stash still sitting on the counter along with a small toy.

"It's fine. Hey, you. Take these. One for eating, one for luck and comfort as your start school."

Bree grinned and murmured her thanks, lifting the plush animal to her lips to kiss.

After Amelia left the kitchen and headed toward the door, Lincoln took a step toward Amelia, but she held up her hand to stop him.

"Just go, Lincoln. Breanne needs you right now."

He watched her a long moment and nodded. "Okay. You're right. But this isn't over yet."

Amelia shook her head and sniffled. "Actually, I think maybe it is."

"Come on, Amelia. You can't be serious. Let's… Look, come away with me." The words came out of nowhere, and he was almost as surprised by them as she seemed to be.

"What?"

"Filming is supposed to wrap up next week, right? I'll have the twins settled in school by then." He stepped close and gently rubbed his hands up and down her arms. "Let's go away somewhere. Just you and me. I'll book us separate rooms and we can talk and—"

"I can't."

He froze, not liking the way she couldn't make eye contact. "Can't? Or don't want to?"

"Lincoln… I should've brought this up sooner. A lot sooner. I-I didn't realize you felt so strongly about not having kids, but now that I see that you do, there's something—"

"What?"

She tucked her head to her chest and moaned softly.

"Izzy. Izzy set me up with Marsali, remember?"

"Yeah, so?"

"So, it was because… I have an appointment in Atlanta at a clinic."

He watched her closely, unable to read the emotions flickering across her face in rapid succession. "Amelia? Are you sick?"

"No… No, I'm not sick."

Relief poured through him. "Thank God. So what are you doing? Some kind of plastic surgery? Honey, you don't need it. You make my heart stop every time I see you now."

She tilted her head to one side, her expression softening. "Thank you. Right back at you," she whispered. "But I'm not having plastic surgery. I'm… getting pregnant."

Shock rolled through him and he told himself he'd misheard her. "*What?*"

"Izzy felt like I'd given up on falling in love and doing things the old-fashioned way, and she was right. I had. So she contacted Marsali and hired her to match me, hoping I'd find someone and fall in love. I agreed to three dates before my appointment on the off chance I'd meet someone I'd want to be with," she said in a rush, arms hugging her front tightly. "I never expected it to be you."

"*Pregnant?*" he asked, still trying to get his brain to work enough to process the news after Breanne's shock from earlier. "You're telling me you're going to a clinic to be—"

"Yes. The first appointment is an assessment and to go over expectations and guidelines, but if things go well, I'll move forward with the procedure. I was planning to cancel it. Because of us. But hearing you say you don't want kids…"

He took a step back, forcing air into his tight chest and feeling much the same as he had while waiting on Breanne to take the test. What had she called it? A panic attack? "Why didn't you say anything before now?"

"What was I supposed to say, Lincoln? We haven't dated that long. Should I have told you on the first date? How would that have gone? Nice to see you again, Lincoln. I know I broke your heart twenty years ago, but would you like to get me pregnant?"

"Um… Dad?"

He closed his eyes and bit back a silent curse when Breanne reentered the room in time to hear Amelia's statement. He could feel his daughter's gaze boring a hole in his back and turned to find her staring at the two of them. "Bree, I'll be there in a second. Just… wait by Amelia's door, please."

Breanne didn't move for a long moment but then did as ordered and disappeared once more. "Amelia—"

"Lincoln, just *go*. You've had enough to deal with tonight and it's not completely over yet."

"That's it? We find each other again and I don't get a say in this plan of yours? The time we've been together meant what to you, exactly?"

Amelia met his gaze with a look that took his breath away and broke his heart all over again.

"It meant everything. I love you, Lincoln. I never

stopped loving you all of these years, and nothing would make me happier than to turn that love into a baby of our own, but if you're so set against it… This is a deal breaker for me. I want kids. You don't. Since we can't agree on this, how can we possibly have a future together?"

Chapter 14

Lincoln stared out at his backyard the following evening after his third call to Amelia went to voicemail. He'd texted her last night after he and Breanne had returned home and asked Amelia to call him on any break she'd had during the day today, but so far all he'd received was radio silence.

"Hey. Everything okay?" Mac asked from his deck. "The food should be here in an hour or so."

The last thing Lincoln felt like doing was socializing, but the evening wasn't about him or his moods and all about the twins' journey to college tomorrow. Since they were packing up the truck and doing last-minute things, Mac had offered to host everyone at his house for dinner and had ordered from the kids' favorite Italian restaurant. "Yeah, we should have everything loaded up and done by then."

"Dad?"

Lincoln turned and found Breanne standing in the doorway to the kitchen, her ex-boyfriend, Jaxon, behind her.

"Can we talk for a minute?" Bree asked.

Lincoln stood and took the conversation in the privacy of the kitchen rather than outside, where they might be overheard. He had to give the boy credit for standing his ground when Lincoln approached, even though Jax looked as pale as the white baseboard behind him. "What's up?"

"Sir, I just… Bree told me what happened. I wanted to come over and… apologize. And to say that if she had been… Sir, I wouldn't have left. I would've stayed and been a dad whether we were together or not. I just wanted you to know that."

Jax was the son of a single mom who'd done a great job raising the boy on her own. Still, the kid knew what it was like growing up without a father, and even though the words were easy to say after the fact when the test was negative, Lincoln sensed the kid meant what he said. "Yeah, well, let this be a lesson to both of you. Sex is a big deal and comes with consequences you'd better be prepared for. Understood?"

"Understood, sir."

Lincoln held out his hand and Jax took it, but Lincoln also gave the kid the parental eye that made it clear Jax had better be respecting Breanne and making better choices from now on. Breanne had already received that lecture, though Lincoln knew it had probably fallen on eighteen-year-old ears. Hopefully the pregnancy scare would at least have an effect for a while and temper any such behavior that would lead to a second scare. He couldn't play the hypocrite, though. He'd been young and stupid once, too. To be honest, it was how he and Jill had wound up with the twins.

"Is it okay if Jax and I walk to get ice cream?"

Breanne said. "One last time? He leaves for school tomorrow, too. I'll be back in time for dinner at Mac's. Dessert first?"

"Just ice cream," he stated drolly, earning a blush from his daughter. "And don't be late. Mac's doing a good thing for you two. Plus I'd like to spend some time with you myself before you leave."

Breanne nodded and rose to her tiptoes to kiss his cheek.

"I won't be long. I love you, Daddy."

He wrapped her in his arms and breathed deeply. "I love you, too, kiddo."

"Is Amelia coming tonight? You invited her, didn't you?"

He and Breanne had talked the entire drive home last evening after leaving her car parked at the pharmacy until this morning. During their talk, Breanne had told him what Amelia had said regarding her desire for motherhood, his daughter adding that Amelia would make an awesome mother. "No. No, she isn't. We said a lot last night, bug. I'm not sure she wants to see me again."

Breanne gave him a look reminiscent of her mother's and shook her head.

"She does, Daddy. Trust me. Call her and ask her to come. You can talk after dinner. You always say Bren and I don't talk to you enough. Tell her the same thing and really listen."

"There may not be a way around this wall, Bree. Now go get your ice cream and stop giving your old man orders."

Jax grinned at the statement but Breanne just stood there, unmoving.

"Dad, she *really* likes you. And you really like her and you've been *so happy* these last few weeks. Everybody's noticed. If this is about me and what happened—"

"Honey, it's not about you. It has nothing to do with you."

"Are you sure? I mean, I can see why you'd be uncomfortable with a grandkid older than one of your own kids, but you're not going to be a grandfather now, so you shouldn't be weirded out by becoming a dad again."

"Bree—"

"When Bren and I are gone, you're going to be lonely in this big house by yourself. You know you are."

Lincoln inhaled in a struggle for patience. "I thought maybe I'd travel. See the world. I haven't had the chance to do that kind of thing."

"Alone? Don't you want Amelia to go with you?"

"Bree—"

"Dad."

"Honey, Amelia and I are in two very different phases of life."

"Why does it have to be that way? You love her. Don't say you don't. "

"I… do love her. But traveling is hard when you're packing around a baby."

Breanne crossed her arms over her chest.

"What?" he asked when he realized he was garnering one of those looks again.

"You and this traveling thing. I don't get it. You hate vacations."

"What? I do not."

"Yeah, you do. You're a borderline workaholic who's always said how you hate airports and hotels and not being home. *You* say when you live at the beach, you don't need vacations."

He had said those things. And hearing them repeated back to him at this moment kind of bit the big one. Traveling was pretty much a way to fill the time between school breaks when the kids would come home to visit. "Maybe I don't want to work as much, ever think of that?"

"Fine. Go and take Amelia."

"Bree—"

"You want to travel and she wants kids *if* she can have them. Something's gotta give, right? So compromise! You can travel until she gets pregnant, and after the baby comes, you can travel when I'm on my school breaks and you pay me *very well* to babysit," she said with a tilt of her chin. "Uncle Carter can pitch in sometimes like you've always done with Piper. Or Bren. We'll all help. What's your excuse now?"

Lincoln faltered. Because with those statements, he didn't really have one.

"Dad? Is this about Mom? Or me and Bren and Mom?"

Lincoln wasn't sure this was a conversation he should be having with teenagers. "Breanne—"

"It bothered me at first, okay? You dating. It seemed weird and wrong. Bren said I was crazy for letting it get to me because it's been three years since Mom died and… he was right. You've been so happy, and after talking with Amelia and getting to know her, I can see why you like her. She's really nice, and if you're going to date someone, it should be her."

"I'm glad you think so," he said. "But don't ever

think you can't come to me to talk about anything, Breanne."

Breanne closed her eyes briefly and nodded.

"I *know*, Daddy. But sometimes a girl needs another girl to talk to."

The air rushed out of his lungs and Lincoln felt dazed by the observation. Why hadn't he thought of that? Considered that? "I'm sorry your mom isn't here for you, sweetheart."

"Me, too," Breanne said, her voice growing thick. "But Amelia *is* here… And even though I don't know her like you do, I think she'd make an awesome second mom, and you're crazy if you end things because she wants a baby. You're old but not *that* old."

"She's right, Dad," Brendan said from the hallway, where he lurked with Carter, who carried Piper in his arms, asleep on his shoulder.

The sight brought out feelings Lincoln wasn't expecting. Yeah, the late nights and diaper years were hard but they were brief, and the kids in front of him were proof that those years flew by. Babies became toddlers and little girls like the one Carter carried. Then they became teenagers like the ones standing in front of him, legal adults.

"You deserve to be happy," Brendan said.

"And so does Amelia," Breanne added with a pointed stare.

She did. And while he stood there staring at the love looking back at him, Lincoln realized how selfish of a person he'd be to keep her from experiencing this for herself. The cuddles and sweetness and even the arguments. "Okay, okay, I see the error in my ways. No need to gang up on me."

Lincoln moved through the crowd assembled inside of his house to get his keys from the bowl on the entry table.

"You going after her?" Carter asked.

"She won't take my calls or return my texts, so, yeah."

"Take flowers. Or a ring," Breanne said.

Lincoln stopped in his tracks and turned, noting the men surrounding her all looked at Breanne the same way he did.

Breanne shrugged and returned the stare with an expression Lincoln treasured because it was such a *Jill* look.

"Well, you know what you want, don't you? There's no time to waste if she wants a baby," Breanne said.

An incredulous huff rumbled out of Lincoln before he walked out the door despite the shouts following him, asking what he planned to do.

They'd find out—as soon as he found Amelia and figured it out for himself.

Chapter 15

The morning after the breakup, Amelia had arrived at work bleary-eyed and exhausted from her sleepless night to learn the movie had wrapped ahead of schedule when the powers that be decided in the middle of the night that they wanted to shoot the outdoor scenes in Charleston instead. The news came as a welcome surprise since it had given Amelia's dragging behind a chance to go home and pack a bag and go to Izzy's home in Carolina Cove to crash and cry from her breaking heart. Maybe by the time the production team returned to Wilmington, Amelia would have pulled herself together.

Her home had always been a sanctuary, but Lincoln's presence in it as they'd realized their demise had left it feeling dark and unwelcoming. Hiding out at Izzy's and ignoring Lincoln's phone calls and texts had taken some doing.

Lincoln had called multiple times, texted several more, but she hadn't responded, knowing there was no use in doing so. There was nothing left to say.

In fact, this was why she'd left town after their first breakup. Because she could barely breathe from the pain as it was, and she was sure if Lincoln tried, he could convince her to change her mind. Convince her that she didn't need or desire a child as long as she had him.

But she did. She'd love nothing more than a baby boy or girl with Lincoln's dark eyes and heart-stopping smile. She couldn't be with him and not want his baby.

She also knew that with every passing moment and every cycle she wasted at this point, her chances to conceive grew even more unlikely.

"Turn or you're gonna burn," Izzy said, her voice muffled from where her face was lying atop her arms as she sunbathed on the sand.

Amelia left her beach chair and crawled the length of her towel to lie on her stomach, wondering how she'd allowed herself to become such a sad sack. She had to prepare herself. Get ready to be a mom. It wouldn't be easy but she could do it and would do it happily.

"Look, I know it sucks and you're hurt and angry but you still have one more fix-up with Marsali."

"Bite your tongue. Use that matchup for yourself," Amelia told her. "I certainly don't want it."

Izzy rose up onto her elbows and stared at Amelia, squinting against the sun until she found her sunglasses and propped them on her nose. When Izzy continued to stare, Amelia sighed. "What?"

"You're still going to Atlanta, aren't you?"

"Of course I am. Why wouldn't I? It takes time to get through the exams and then the procedure itself. And that's if it takes on the first try. There's no reason to wait, and since I now have a few extra days, I'm going to make the most of them. Besides, you said you'd support me, remember? I went along with your plan and it didn't work. Now it's time for you to suck it up and encourage me."

Izzy used one long finger to lower the glasses on her nose so Amelia could see her eyes.

"I support you. We can raise the kid together. It'll likely have issues because we're both a mess, but, hey, that's what therapy is for, right?"

"You're mean."

"Just stating facts, doll. Tube-kid will have hang-ups, so you'll need to be prepared. Therapy is a must. I mean, look at me. My only deficit is that I'm the baby of the family, but you *know* how I am with my sister issues. You're fooling yourself if you don't go ahead and open that savings account now."

"All right, all right. I'll start a therapy fund for when they need it. Satisfied?"

"Yes," Izzy said with a grin and a shove of her glasses.

"But you have to stop calling my baby Tube-kid."

"Cocktail baby?"

"Izzy!"

"Tubey?"

"I'm going to strangle you."

"Glass-patterned baldness?"

"Last warning. I mean it!"

"Okay. Okay. No, wait, I have one more—"

"Say it and die."

"When do you leave for your appointment?" Izzy asked sweetly.

Glad her friend had stopped with the name-calling,

Amelia closed her eyes and made herself more comfortable on the towel. "Five a.m. tomorrow."

"And you're sure you don't want me to come with you?"

"And listen to you make up names the entire way? No. And because I actually do want to leave at five and beat the traffic into Atlanta." Izzy was a great artist. She was not a morning person, however, and taking her along meant any number of delays along the way. "I'll call you after I get there and settle into my hotel. I plan to use the extra days off to have a spa day and try to catch up on the sleep I've missed because of filming before I see the doctors."

"Fun. You should definitely do the spa day. Expectant mamas need pampering, and you have to do it while you can still lie on your stomach."

Amelia shook her head at Izzy's statement, a wry smile pulling at her lips. "Thank you."

"For harassing you out of love?"

"For letting me stay at your place to cry it out and taking the day off today."

"Considering I kinda got you hooked up with Lincoln in a roundabout way, it's the least I could do."

"You're right. My heart is broken because of you. It is all your fault," Amelia said. "Thanks."

"So how are you going to handle things? Are you just going to ghost him, or do you think you'll talk to him eventually?"

Amelia turned her face down atop her hands to hide her trembling lips and the tears stinging her eyes. "We're done, Izzy. Best to just cut my losses while I can."

"You know what you could do?"

"What?"

"Pick a baby daddy who looks like Lincoln."

"You can't be serious?"

"What? I'm just saying. Imagine Lincoln's surprise if you run into him again with the kid in tow. Now *that* would be funny!"

Izzy's ornery laughter brought a smile to Amelia's lips despite her efforts to discourage her friend's less-than-friendly comments.

Still… maybe it was something to consider?

Because when it came to having a child, she couldn't think of anyone else she'd want her baby to look like.

FIVE O'CLOCK THE NEXT MORNING, Amelia was buzzing down River Road on her way out of town when she remembered that she'd forgotten to pack her computer charger when she'd grabbed it for her mad dash to Izzy's. She groaned at the inconvenience of having to make the unexpected stop but parked outside her building for the quick run inside.

She got off the elevator and had taken four steps down the hall when she spotted the legs sprawled out from her closed door. Amelia slowed her steps, gaze searching as she inched closer and realized the long legs belonged to Lincoln.

He'd slept here? All night?

Why not in his car?

At his house?

Oh, she didn't have time for this. More importantly, she didn't have the energy or emotional stamina. "Lincoln?"

He didn't stir. He really was asleep.

She moved closer and knelt beside him, only then

spotting the bouquet of hydrangeas and jasmine on the ground by his hip. "Come on, Sleeping Beauty, wake up." She gently shook his shoulder. "Lincoln?"

He awoke with a startled jolt, grabbing her hand.

"Hey," he said, squinting and blinking as though trying to focus. "You're finally home. What time is it?"

"Five fifteen. In the morning, Lincoln. Have you been here all night?"

He closed his eyes drowsily and she wondered if he was actually awake yet. "Lincoln?"

"Sleeping Beauty doesn't wake up until he's kissed," he murmured.

"Yeah, well, Sleeping Beauty shouldn't be sleeping here. It's a wonder my neighbors didn't call the cops on you. Lincoln?" Seriously? He wasn't going to respond until she kissed him? "Oh, for pity's sake."

Since it might be the last time she ever got the opportunity to kiss him, she leaned over to press a quick kiss to his lips only to gasp when his hands shot up to grasp her shoulders. He kept her there, his lips fastening on to hers with all of the intensity and chemistry they'd shared from day one. The kiss deepened until she had to end it due to lack of air.

"You taste minty," he murmured, his long fingers tangled in her hair. "I like it."

She liked this. This sleepy-eyed, hair-pulling, incredibly sexy Lincoln. Amelia crouched over him, hands on his chest for balance, body quaking. How was it possible to want someone like this, even though it hurt so much? "Don't do this to me, Lincoln. Please. I can't—"

He kissed her again, stopping her complaint.

"Invite me in."

"Mm. No. No, I don't— I *can't*. I just stopped to pick up a charger that I forgot. I'm on my way to Atlanta."

"I was afraid you'd already left. I've been trying to get ahold of you for days, but you wouldn't answer or return my calls, and the news said the filming had ended early. I've been out of my mind wondering if I was too late. I had to get the kids off to college yesterday, but I came straight back here hoping to catch you and talk to you before you—"

"You're *not* going to talk me out of it. Because of my age and issues, I know I might not be able to have a baby, and if that happens, I'll accept it, but I have to *try*, Lincoln. I *want* to try. I want a *baby*."

His hand tightened in her hair a bit more, and a shiver seared her nerve endings as he locked gazes with her.

"That's why I'm here, sweetheart. Because if you want to have a baby, I want it to be with me."

Chapter 16

Lincoln waited for Amelia to respond, barely able to breathe due to the fist in his stomach. Her doorstep wasn't the place to have this conversation, but he couldn't bring himself to wait even longer. Not when he'd agonized and paced and worried himself into exhaustion waiting on her to appear.

He'd gotten so desperate he'd Googled sperm banks in Atlanta, but due to the laws, he wasn't able to get any information when he called trying to find her.

"What?"

Lincoln stared into her beautiful gaze and struggled to clear the fog in his brain. He needed his wits about him to argue all the reasons why she needed to give him a third chance. "Sweetheart, when you mentioned a baby... all I could think of was that I was almost a *grandfather*."

"You would've been a young grandfather."

He narrowed his gaze, earning a slight smile from her. Having slept against her door all night, he now felt every ache and pain, and he definitely didn't feel as young as he used to feel. "Yeah, well, in a few years, I'm likely to *be* a grandfather and… you talking about babies threw me, and Bree's pregnancy scare threw me even more. All of it crashed in on me. Dating and babies and *you*. It's fast for someone who's moved at a snail's pace the last twenty years, raising two families."

"I'm sure it is. I'm sorry I've made things even more difficult."

"No. No, don't be sorry," he said, using his hold on her to settle her weight entirely against him so that she sat beside him on her doormat. "Because the thing of it is, all of this—namely you—has made me feel more alive than I have in a very long time."

"It has?"

His gaze lowered to her mouth and he watched as she flicked a tongue over her lips in response. "It takes a lot of practice to make a baby."

Her face colored with a blush, and he ran his thumb under the fullness of her lower lip.

"Um… We should… Maybe we should go get some coffee to finish this conversation?"

"No. I want an answer, Amelia. Right here. Right now."

"Lincoln, I can't help but think you feel pressured because of me and my body's timetable. Are you sure this is what *you* want?"

"Yes, sweetheart. I know what I want, and if you're going to have a baby, I want it to be with me. No one else."

A strange look flitted across her face.

"What? What's the matter now?"

"I'm afraid I might be confusing things. Are you saying you want to… *donate*? To the cause?"

"What? No. Well, yes, technically," he said, cocking his head with a wry grin, "but no. Ahhh, I'm bumbling this."

"Would coffee help?"

A rough chuckle started low in his chest and rumbled out and he groaned at the pain it caused. "Coffee would be great, but after sleeping propped against your door, I think I'd have to crawl in to get it."

"Oh. *Oh, Lincoln.*"

A laugh erupted out of her, softening the worry lines he'd probably put there. He tugged her low once more and kissed her, softly, sweetly, lingering over the contact and taste of her. "Amelia, I'm saying I love you. I also never stopped loving you and I want to be with you. Will you marry me?"

"M-marry you?"

"You want my baby, you're going to have to make an honest man of me." He released her long enough to dig the velvet case and the ring he'd purchased on his mad dash to her house several evenings ago out of his pocket.

Amelia gasped at the sight of the ring box and her eyes filled with tears.

"That's for me?"

"If you don't like it, we can go back and pick out something else."

She held the box closed when he tried to open it and shook her head.

"It's beautiful. It's *perfect.*"

He brushed her hand away and fished the ring from the satin folds, sliding it onto her finger. A tear trickled down her cheek and she hurried to wipe it away as she stared at it. "Is that a yes?" he asked, watching her every move and loving her emotional response. It was as honest and telling as she was.

Her nod was rapid and wobbly but affirmative, and her smile left him feeling like someone had sucked the air out of his lungs.

"Yes. Yes, I would love to marry you. To make babies with you. Oh, Lincoln, I love you."

She kissed him with all the happiness and frustration and pent-up emotion he'd experienced the last few days without her. He pulled her across his lap, cradled her against him, and they celebrated the moment as the sky began to lighten with the first sign of the sunrise. After several more kisses and a few whispers about what he couldn't wait to do with her, he pulled away, groaning. "We have to get inside."

"Now?"

He chuckled at her question. "You have an appointment to cancel."

Chapter 17

Ten months later

TWO DAYS after Amelia's thirty-ninth birthday, Lincoln held her hand as she pushed their baby into the world. She fell back against Lincoln's chest, grateful for the support of his loving arms and chest surrounding her.

"It's a boy," the midwife said, her eyes smiling from behind her glasses. "Ten fingers and toes, Mama Bear. All looks good. Rest for a minute and catch your breath."

A soft sob ripped out of Amelia's chest, one of relief and love and the overwhelming gratitude for such a blessing. She and Lincoln had wasted no time on making things official. Since it was Amelia's first time tying the knot, Izzy had insisted they do it right, and when Lincoln realized that she did have a certain wedding in mind, he'd hired Marsali's best friend and miracle-working wedding planner, Eliza Bellefonte, to create Amelia's perfect beach wedding at sunset.

It had been yet another example of Lincoln's love for her, that of withstanding the fuss and preparation when she knew he would've been happy with a trip to the courthouse.

Eliza had truly outdone herself. The woman had weddings down to a science, and somehow she'd been able to pull off Lincoln's one demand—the ceremony had to take place within two weeks. Thirteen days later, Amelia's father had walked her down the aisle to where Lincoln stood and given her to the man she'd loved all her life.

Piper had made an adorable flower girl, Izzy was Amelia's maid of honor, Breanne a bridesmaid, and Carter and Brendan had stood in as Lincoln's best man and groomsman. As the sun set and the sky filled with a dazzling array of colors, Lincoln sealed their vows with a kiss that had left her toes curling into the sand.

Amelia closed her eyes and pictured it now, the way Lincoln had stood there so tall and broad. The sweet hugs and kisses from his children as they accepted her as one of them. She knew she'd never be their mom, but she would do her very best to honor the woman who was and fill the void left behind by her passing.

"What are you thinking about?" Lincoln asked.

A contraction built in her belly and she smoothed her palms over the taut surface. "Our wedding. How beautiful. They're next," she said, smiling. "Wait and see."

"Who's next?"

"Okay, Mama, you ready to go again?"

Amelia nodded to the midwife when the contraction grew in strength and intensity. She forgot all about her friends and focused on the physical act of breathing and the pain shredding her body.

Due to her age and the endometriosis, her doctor had agreed to fertility medication that sometimes produced multiple births. In their case, they'd been given a double blessing. The second of which was now — "Owww," she said, groaning and crying and struggling to fight through the pain.

"Your baby girl is stubborn," Lincoln said, whispering the words in her ear. "Just wait until she's a teenager and you two butt heads. Come on, Amelia, push. You can do this. Come on."

She closed her eyes and clenched her teeth and bore down hard, but it still took three more minutes of pushing before their daughter followed her brother into the room. When she did, the L and D suite was filled with baby cries that were the sweetest music ever.

"Congratulations," the midwife said.

Lincoln gently hugged her tight before he extracted himself from behind her on the bed to take photos as the nurses cleaned up the babies and did the initial assessments. Amelia leaned heavily into the pillow at her head and tried to catch her breath, tired and elated and overwhelmed by everything as the post-birth process took place.

She opened her eyes in time to see Lincoln lean over the bed. He brushed the tears of pain from her cheeks and gave her a slow, sweet kiss, and she reveled in the feel of his touch, smiling when she thought of his statement that morning outside of her condo door.

The baby making was definitely the fun part. This? Not so much.

"You were amazing, sweetheart."

She lost herself in the love shining out of Lincoln's gaze, happier than she could ever remember being.

"Here you go," the midwife said, approaching the bed carrying one baby while a nurse followed with the other. "One for each of you. Do we have names?"

"We haven't settled on those yet. We wanted to see them first," Amelia said, taking her pink-hatted daughter into her arms and cradling her next to her chest.

Lincoln received his son, and Amelia was struck at how utterly sexy he was with his arms bulging as he held the tiny bundle of blue.

This. This was what she'd wanted.

Him. Them. This precious moment that represented all the love she had to give and the family she had taken on when she'd taken her vows. Breanne and Brendan had thrived in college, making the dean's list both semesters. They'd just finished their finals and had moved back to Carolina Cove in time to find summer jobs and help with the babies, both of them excited to meet their baby brother and sister. For the last several weeks, their home had been filled with laughter and fun, baby showers, and last-minute preparations. With all the kids under one roof, she knew it would be bursting at the seams as their family got to know one another and settled into a routine.

Amelia pressed a soft kiss to her daughter's wrinkled forehead and whispered her love to the scrunched-up little face. Lincoln sat next to her on the bed, and after a bit, he asked if she wanted to meet her son. Lincoln gave her their son for the swap, and she held both babies in her arms, looking up to find Lincoln struggling to contain his emotions. "What? What is it?"

"You," he whispered, clearing his throat gruffly as he bent over them and pressed a kiss on her temple. "If not for their stubborn mama, I would've missed out on this, and now I can't imagine not seeing you like this, with them. I love you, Amelia." His voice choked as he whispered the words, and tears trickled down Amelia's cheeks as she watched her husband cradle their little family, his arms wrapped around hers.

Lincoln kissed her again, lingering over the caress before shifting to hold his daughter for the first time. "Hey, you," he said, settling her against him. "Let me see you. What's your name, huh? Who are you? Tell me."

I hope you enjoyed reading Amelia and Lincoln's second chance at love story. Carter and Eliza's book is available now. How does the single dad handle his interest in the fiercely independent Eliza? Are they ready to follow Marsali's rules? Read RULES OF ENGAGEMENT or get a sneak peek at an excerpt below:

RULES OF ENGAGEMENT EXCERPT

Wedding planner Eliza Bellefonte smiled at the happy couple and watched as they made their way onto the dance floor inside the tent dominating the seaside location.

Beneath the crisp white canvas, three hundred natural bamboo chairs with white cushions matched white-draped tables. Atop those were sand-colored runners twisted with fairy lights and soft teal ribbon, assorted white flowers, and white candles. The displays ran the length of the tables and twinkled in time with the ten thousand lights in various sizes stretched above their heads. Thankfully the sides of the tent were open, allowing the sea breeze to lower the heat created by the press of people, candles, and lights.

The very young, very spoiled bride had insisted on taupe and white for the foundation to make it more "beachy," even though she'd also demanded the tent have a floor to keep all that awful sand contained. Eliza remembered hearing that request—the hundredth or so at that point—and biting her lip to keep the smile pinned to her face.

Why bother with a beach wedding if sand wasn't a welcome guest?

But the bride was always right, even if she was neurotic about sand—on the beach.

Eliza forced her thoughts away from the couple of the day and focused on the cashier's check processing its way into her account via her bank's phone app. One must never be too cautious, and this bridezilla had made Eliza a little too nervous with last-minute switches that always came with a comment about not paying if it wasn't "just right."

Eliza had contracts in place to cover her own interests, but negative social media or having to get her attorney involved however briefly could end in disaster for her business. It paid to be overly cautious—and overly accommodating. None of it mattered so long as she got paid.

When the darling's daddy had handed over the last of the payment this morning, Eliza had taken no chances and excused herself to quickly snap a photo and send it on its way. After the months of planning, ordering, preparing… she'd earned every penny and then some.

"Gorgeous," Marsali Jones said. "As always."

Eliza turned to find her best friend of the last six years standing behind her, another woman at Marsali's side. "Hey," she said with a smile after muting the mic she wore, leaning into Marsali's quick hug. "I didn't see your name on the list. What are you doing here?"

Given that Marsali was a professional matchmaker and friends with Hollywood A-lister Oliver Beck, it wasn't unusual for Marsali to appear at functions with a number of Wilmywood's movie production crowds. Bridezilla's groom was part of that movie-making group but—

"I'm Amelia's plus-one today," Marsali said, introducing Eliza to Amelia Porter, a set designer. "When she said she hadn't been able to get in touch with you and her fiancé couldn't make it, I volunteered to come and convince you to pull off a mini-miracle for her."

"A miracle?" Oh, boy. *That's* why Amelia's name sounded familiar. She'd been dodging the woman's calls for the last several days. "Ah, now I remember," she said. "As you can see, I've been a little busy, but I'd planned to return your call once all of this was over," Eliza said, waving a hand at the interior and crowd. "When's the date?"

Amelia exchanged a glance with Marsali before making eye contact with Eliza.

"Two weeks," the woman said, grimacing. "I know. It's asking *a lot* because it's a huge rush, but if I want a wedding instead of just a date at the courthouse, it's the only way. I'm… kind of on a time schedule and we don't want to take a year to plan something. But we want small and intimate, special," she added, "since it's my first and only."

Eliza ignored the *first and only* comment and focused

on the schedule. Two weeks? With her calendar booked solid? She glanced at Marsali.

"You and I both know you can totally pull it off. *And*," Marsali added, "they'll happily pay you whatever it takes to make it happen in that time frame."

"After seeing how amazing this is, I really want you to plan it, Eliza," Amelia said. "Please. Say yes."

Eliza stared out at the large area scattered with lounges and love seats tossed with white and soft teal pillows. Every table held crystal and china and vases of jasmine, rustic and custom-made driftwood holders cradling tea lights, and glittering seashells. Outside, tulle billowed in the breeze, looped across the custom arch and anchored with roping and gigantic flower arrangements.

Like Amelia, so many wanted the perfect wedding but had no clue of the effort it took to make such things happen. The venue, lighting, seating, props, gowns, catering, band, staff, fittings, setup and takedown labor. No matter how simple a bride *said* she wanted a wedding to be, it *always* turned into more.

Weddings were a production, and the deeper the pockets the bride and groom—or their parents—had, the bigger and more elaborate things tended to get. But Eliza had yet to fail her clients. Whatever they wanted, they got. After all, happy customers fueled her healthy bank account and the reassurance those numbers gave her state of mind.

"Eliza?" Marsali nudged her arm. "I'll help however I can. I know it's late notice but… I'd consider it a personal favor. They've got a *great* personal story, and it deserves a celebration the likes of which only you can pull off. Please?"

Eliza shot both women a glance before she inhaled and opened the book she carried everywhere with her. She had copies of her copies, because when she couldn't find something digitally, she always fell back on her trusty paper bible of wedding information. "Two weeks," she murmured. "What day?"

"A weekend would be best but… any evening. You make it work," Amelia said. "And we'll make it work, too."

Wow. Now that was an unusual comment. Usually the bride had one date in mind and refused to budge from it, demanding the world stop whirling and shift around her date accordingly. "I… have a Thursday evening open two and a half weeks from now. My weekends are taken. Sorry."

"Ink us in," Amelia said with a happy smile, her hands clasped in front of her like she wanted to dance and tried to contain her excitement.

"Ink, huh? We haven't discussed my fees," Eliza murmured.

"If you can do something like this on a small scale in that time frame? Ink," Amelia said, nodding her head to confirm her words while giving Eliza a steady look.

Yeah. This had taken fourteen months to plan. Two weeks? Sure, no problem. "Do you have your gown?"

"No."

"Venue?"

"No."

"Color scheme?"

Eliza glanced up and found Amelia beginning to look a bit wild-eyed and panicked. A soft laugh left her chest, and Eliza shook her head and snapped the book closed. She really needed to investigate panicked-bride hazard pay. "Meet me after the reception is over and we'll talk specifics then."

"But you'll do it?" Amelia said.

Eliza agreed with a nod, rattled off the Thursday evening date just to confirm it, and Amelia and Marsali gave her quick hugs in response.

"Thank you. Thank you *so* much. Oh, I have to call Lincoln and tell him we have a date. I'm so excited! Excuse me."

Marsali remained after Amelia hurried away, and once the woman was out of hearing range, Eliza stared up at her taller friend and lifted a single eyebrow high. "Are you trying to put me in an early grave?"

Marsali laughed and wrapped an arm around Eliza's shoulders, squeezing.

"Nope. I'm trying to show you that there are actually special couples out there who have the forever kind of love, and Amelia and Lincoln are one of them."

"Uh-huh."

Marsali released Eliza and stepped in front of her to get her full attention.

"You amaze me. *How* do you make a living planning weddings that look like something out of a fairy tale or catalog shoot when you don't even believe in love?"

"Easy. It's called financial security."

"You're so jaded."

"Yeah, well, you're delusional, Miss Matchmaker. These two?" she said, lowering her voice to a cautious whisper. "I give them nine months and *that's* being generous."

"Eliza. That's awful."

"Hey, I've been doing this since I was sixteen. The

rose-colored glasses have long since shattered. I've learned the signs, and trust me… they don't have it."

"What signs?"

"He's twice her age and it's his second marriage because Flirty Child Bride broke up the first, *and* there's no prenup. He was also in the bar last night with his hands all over a waitress, while *she*—"

"No need to continue," Marsali interrupted. "I like my naive state where I can still believe in love. Don't ruin it."

Eliza chuckled at her sweet friend's expression and hooked their arms, tugging Marsali toward the bar. "That's because you're in love with love. And a Hollywood hottie."

"Stop it. I am not."

"Hmm. Lie to yourself if you like. Me? I see how you eye your *Ollie*."

"Shh. Keep your voice down," Marsali said. "He has other friends here, you know."

"So you admit it?" Eliza asked Marsali.

"Absolutely not. Oliver is… a friend. Who, I might add, lives in LA while I'm here. Besides that, he only sees me as Mac's little sister."

"Which is why Mac's little sister needs to focus on her *best-selling* book—congrats again, by the way—and nothing else."

"Thank you. The flowers were lovely. You shouldn't have."

"You're welcome."

"But you're still cynical," Marsali muttered.

Eliza shifted her weight on her aching feet and wished once again the bride hadn't been so anti-sand. The hardwood floor wasn't nearly as forgiving. "I'm realistic. Love gets most everyone to the altar, but it does nothing to keep them married."

"That's called commitment."

"Not arguing there."

"That's it. I'm fixing you up no matter how much you protest. I don't care what you say, I'm going to find the perfect man for you," Marsali said. "He'll sweep you off your feet and you won't know what hit you."

Eliza stared up at her taller friend and shook her head wryly. "Wanna bet?"

CARTER HAYES LEFT HIS HOUSE, crossed his rear deck, and headed next door. Mac's home stood between Carter's and his brother Lincoln's, and ever since moving in, he had acted as the in-between for the three bachelors.

"Hey, you made it. How's Piper?" Mac asked.

Carter jogged up the stairs to Mac's second floor. "Quiet but getting back to her usual self," Carter said. "I reminded her that her cousins will be home for visits and will hang out with her on video chat sometimes until then. She isn't happy but she's adjusting."

Lincoln's twins had left for college a week ago and were settling in, and Piper hated that her cousins wouldn't be around for her first day of kindergarten. Now that she was going to school like the "big kids," she wanted them to be around to acknowledge the fact. "Breanne recommended another friend of hers to babysit," he said, referring to his niece. "They're inside watching a movie."

"*Another* babysitter?"

Carter glared at Mac. "The last one didn't work out."

"What happened?"

"Don't ask."

Mac started chuckling and Carter glared at his friend. "It's not funny."

"Ah, but it is. Little Miss Hottie came on to you, didn't she? I saw her getting out of her convertible in her cheerleading uniform."

Carter swiped a hand over his face and rubbed hard. "That girl had *just* turned sixteen. If Piper *ever*—" He broke off, unsure of what he'd do other than lock his daughter up in her bedroom and not let her out until she was forty.

Some men would've moved on the babysitter without a care for the consequences, but having a daughter of his own *and* not wanting to go to prison for statutory rape, Carter had fired the girl on the spot.

"It's that bad-boy look," Mac stated with a grin. "The muscles, Harley, and tatts? You're the triple crown."

"Bite me. And give me one of those," he said, wagging his fingers for a bottle of water. He'd rather have a beer but these days it paid to have a clear head. Especially when teenage girls were in his house. "Where's Linc?"

"His text said he's finishing up some work but would be over soon."

"He's working crazy hours trying to get a handle on things before he and Amelia get married," Carter said. He wondered if their nightly "guy" ritual would continue after Lincoln tied the knot or if their buddy hang-out sessions would dwindle down to the two remaining bachelors. Time would tell. "How's Marsali?"

He asked the question to get a rise out of Mac, and sure enough, the man drew back and glared at Carter with all the animosity of a friend with a hot sister.

"Watch yourself," Mac said, pointing a finger at Carter.

"Just asking."

"Gentlemen," Lincoln said. "What are we arguing about?"

Lincoln had managed to leave his house and join them without Carter's awareness. "Marsali."

"Carter's hot underage babysitter."

Carter grimaced and shook his head at his older brother. The last thing he needed was Lincoln reverting to old times when he had a right to lecture as his legal guardian. At thirty-three, Carter was a grown man and Lincoln had lost that right.

"Marsali isn't your type," Lincoln said.

"Definitely not," Mac added.

"I don't know about that. She's hot, smart, does her own thing."

"*No,*" Lincoln and Mac said in unison.

"Why not?" he said, just to egg them on. He really wasn't interested in Marsali, though his statements about her hotness were totally accurate. She was a little too... sweet for him, though. And there was the fact she was his buddy's little sis. "You always tell me I'm looking in the wrong places and that's why I've found the wrong women. Maybe Marsali and I—"

"Do you want me to kill you?" Mac demanded. "Keep talking."

Carter surrendered the argument with a chuckle.

"You should know by now I'm not interested. Piper may need a mama but I'm living proof not everyone is cut out for the job."

"Barflies seldom are," Lincoln added with a pointed stare.

Carter didn't comment and the subject changed to Amelia's whereabouts on this humid August evening.

"She's at a wedding for an associate. She wanted me to go but I had to some work to get done. Marsali recommended a wedding planner but she's proven hard to get in touch with."

"Wedding planner, huh? No justice of the peace?" Carter asked, knowing his brother wasn't the kind of guy who liked the fuss.

"It's her first and I want her to get what she wants."

"Eliza's good," Mac said. "If anyone can plan something fast and keep it looking nice, she's the one."

Lincoln's phone bleeped and Carter watched as his brother read the message and smiled.

"What? Amelia sexting you?" Carter asked.

"No, but the girls apparently stayed after the reception to plan our wedding. Amelia needs a ride."

"As does my sister," Mac said, shaking his head while staring at his own phone screen. "Apparently someone gifted them with champagne and they've enjoyed themselves."

"Well, I'm due some entertainment," Carter said, standing when they did. "I'll tag along. Piper's babysitter is good for another two hours."

Mac didn't budge and Carter was aware of his pointed glare. "What?" he asked. "Afraid I'm going to mack on your drunk sister?"

When both Lincoln and Mac glared at him, Carter

sighed. "I'm not into Marsali, okay? She's cute but too sweet for my tastes. I like a little more spunk. I'm just going along for kicks."

Mac's gaze narrowed, but after a moment, he seemed to accept Carter's words as truth, and the three of them made their way through their respective houses to properly lock up before meeting outside of Mac's, where they climbed into his large SUV.

Getting to the hotel didn't take long, and as they entered the lobby, feminine laughter filled the atrium. Carter spotted the ladies immediately, his gaze zeroing in on the brunette sitting with Marsali and Amelia. The woman's smirk drew his attention, and once he was close enough to get a better look, he noted how her dark green eyes sparkled with amusement.

"Ah, there's my handsome man now," Amelia said, giggling. "Hi, future husband."

Lincoln bent over the couch where Amelia sat and bussed a kiss over her lips. Carter watched the exchange, a tug of envy tightening his muscles. For all the talk and bluster and teasing, he envied the love Lincoln had found with Amelia. His brother had been blessed twice over with quality women, whereas Carter had chosen badly and ended up still single and struggling as a single dad.

"Eliza Bellefonte, my fiancé, Lincoln Hayes, and his brother, Carter. I think you know Mac?" Amelia said.

"The bachelors," Marsali said. "You know, it reflects poorly on me that my own brother won't let me match him up," she said. "Or *you*," Marsali said, pointing at Carter and waggling her finger. "You need to hire me."

"I'll find my own match," Mac said to his sister. "And stop harassing my friends."

"That's what I said," the other woman agreed with a nod of her tousled head and lift of her nearly empty glass. "Nice to meet you, though."

Mac chuckled. "Eliza, you're looking… happy."

"That's 'cause the check didn't bounce and Bridezilla's daddy was so happy to get her off his hands he gave us *that* to celebrate," Eliza said, waving a manicured hand toward a huge bottle of Dom. "Oh! And Amelia and I made great progress in planning her two-week wedding."

Cheers went up amongst the women once more, and they downed the last of their drinks as the guys watched with varying degrees of amusement and headshaking.

"Ladies, it's been fun but I have had a long, exhausting day," Eliza said. "Amelia, I'll email you the contract tomorrow."

"Thank you again," Amelia said.

"You got it," Eliza said. "Marsali, girl, we need to stop saying we'll get together for that vacation and actually do it."

"Agreed."

"Eliza, how are you getting home?" Mac asked.

"Not going," Eliza stated, setting her glass on the coffee table in front of them. "Perks of being a wedding planner. I get a room and a write-off when an event ends after a certain time. I just have to get to my room and remember not to skinny-dip in the hot tub on the way," she said, scooting to the edge of the couch cushion.

Eliza wobbled as she got to her feet and, standing closest to her, Carter quickly reached out to steady her.

"Hmm. Hello. Who are you again?"

"Carter Hayes." Carter ignored Mac's glare. His

buddy couldn't claim "off-limits" on both his sister *and* her friend. That just wasn't cool. "Nice to meet you, Eliza," he said, sliding her arm through his. "How about I walk you to your room?"

Download RULES OF ENGAGEMENT

Or read one of Kay's other series listed below:

MAKE ME A MATCH SERIES:

- ROMANCE RESET
- RULES OF ENGAGEMENT
- THE MATCHMAKER'S SECRET
- PERFECTLY MISMATCHED
- BY THE BOOK

MONTANA SECRETS SERIES:

- HEALING HER COWBOY
- IT HAD TO BE YOU
- HERS TO KEEP
- MILLION DOLLAR STANDOFF
- HIS CHRISTMAS WISH
- THEIR SECRET SON

THE SEASIDE SISTERS SERIES:

- THE LAST GOODBYE
- LATTES AND LULLABYES
- MAP OF DREAMS
- WORTH THE RISK
- LOST LOVE FOUND

TAMING THE TULANES SERIES:

- SMALL TOWN SCANDAL
- THEIR SECRET BARGAIN
- CROSSING THE LINE
- THE NANNY'S SECRET
- SOMEONE TO TRUST

THE STONE RIVER SERIES:

- WORTH THE WAIT
- NOT BY SIGHT
- THROUGH THE VALLEY
- LEAD ME NOT
- CHRISTMAS AT HOLLY WOOD
- THEIR CHRISTMAS MIRACLE
- SECOND CHANCES

SMALL TOWN SCANDALS SERIES:

- BRODY'S REDEMPTION
- FALLING FOR HER BOSS
- WITH THIS MAN

SECRET SANTA SERIES:

- SECRET SANTA
- SECRET SANTA II: A CHRISTMAS TO REMEMBER

Books Also Set in Carolina Cove

THE SEASIDE SISTERS SERIES:

- THE LAST GOODBYE
- LATTES AND LULLABYES
- MAP OF DREAMS
- WORTH THE RISK
- LOST LOVE FOUND

Want to read other books set in my fictional coastal town of Carolina Cove? Check out the excerpt of THE LAST GOODBYE:

Dominic Dunn hit his turn signal and waited for a family of five to cross the sidewalk before he turned into the Carolina Cove Inn lot and parked, dread filling his stomach. Just the sight of the happy families and tourists wandering the sidewalks, lounging on restaurant patios, and enjoying the lively Saturday night left him angry. He should've ignored the letter. Ignored his next-door neighbor and best friend, ignored his boss and coworkers who said he had to honor Lisa's last request and come here.

"Mister? You gonna get out?"

The boy's voice startled Dominic and he turned to see a kid around eight years old watching him. The salt-air breeze blowing through the open windows of his car brought with it the smell of fried foods from the restaurants nearby, and seagulls squawked as they flew overhead.

"Mister?"

"Yeah," Dominic said, only then realizing he'd pulled into a parking place and was literally sitting there with his foot on the brake as he debated his choices of whether to throw the new car in reverse and floor it to get out of Carolina Cove as quickly as possible… or stay the prepaid two weeks Lisa had booked for him before her death.

"Doesn't look like it. Are you drunk?"

A rough-sounding chuckle left his chest. "Do you get a lot of drunk people here?"

"Sometimes."

"I see. Well, I'm not drunk. Just trying to decide if I want to stay here."

"Oh. You got a reservation?"

Did the kid ever stop asking questions? A memory formed, that of his son, Elijah, at the same age. "Yeah, I do."

"Then why don't you wanna stay?"

Dominic glanced at the clock and noted the time. If he left now, he'd add another six hours to his drive from Atlanta. Not how he wanted to spend what was left of the day. Maybe he should spend the night and head back to Atlanta first thing in the morning? "You've convinced me. I guess I will stay."

"I'll show you the way to the office."

"Do your parents know you're out here near the street? You're awfully young to be wandering about on your own."

The kid's shoulders squared and he lifted his chin to a defiant angle.

"I'm almost ten."

He looked younger, maybe because of his small stature. "Well, almost ten or not, there are a lot of strangers milling around, and it's not safe for kids these days. Are you visiting?" He sounded like an old man talking about "the good old days" but it was true. What kind of parent just let their kid wander the streets in a beach town full of people, some of whom probably waited on the opportunity to grab a kid and head out of town?

"No. I live here. You coming or not?"

The kid had spunk, Dominic had to give him that.

He rolled up the windows of the Porsche 911, killing the powerful engine with another press of a button. He felt a little conspicuous driving the flashy car, but he had to admit he loved the power. Just like Lisa knew he would.

He opened the door and climbed out of the low vehicle, yet another thing to get used to after driving a family-friendly SUV for so many years.

"Wow. You're tall. My mom is too. I hope I'm tall when I grow up."

Dominic locked the car and fell into step behind the boy. "I see the sign for the office. You can head home if you like."

"No. I need to check in anyway." The kid turned around and walked backward, rolling his eyes in classic kid fashion. "Or my mom will freak out and call the police again."

Again? "Does that happen a lot?"

"Her calling the police or freaking out?"

"Take your pick."

"Yeah."

Yeah to… both? Dom bit back another chuckle. Given the kid's intrepid personality, he probably kept his mom busy.

The kid flipped face-forward and Dom watched as the boy ran up the two steps leading to the office. He yanked open the door.

"Mom! Reservation!"

Dom noted the wide southern porch with its rocking chairs and a few chairs and tables before he followed the kid inside, well able to see why Lisa had liked the inn so much if the porch and office interior were anything by which to judge. It was her style of decorating. Beachy but understated.

The office walls were a soft gray with blue and sand-colored accents. There was a comfortable-looking couch and chair in the waiting area, a rope swing hanging from the ceiling in front of a painted mural of the beach and ocean behind, and on the opposite side, a coffee bar, popcorn machine, and snack area with a couple of parlor-type tables and chairs.

"Mom!"

"Samuel, how many times have I told you? No yelling. Inside voice," a woman stated as she appeared from a hallway behind the chest-high desk.

Dominic stilled, uncomfortable with the stomach-punching fact he found her beautiful. He'd guess her age to be early to mid-thirties, tall like her son said, at around five eight. Her auburn hair was scooped back and held at her nape, but curly tendrils framed her face and highlighted striking eyes that matched the blue of the ocean painting behind the check-in area.

"But, Mom, you have a reservation and sometimes don't hear me."

"A— Oh," she said, locking gazes with Dominic. "Sorry about that. Welcome to Carolina Cove Inn. I'm Ireland Cohen, the manager."

He forced himself to focus on her name rather than her beauty. "Ireland? Like the country?"

"Yes."

"Unusual name."

"Unusual family," she said by way of explanation. She flashed them both a smile. "I hope I didn't keep you waiting too long?"

"Not at all. Samuel kept me company."

"Mom, you should see his cool car! I'll bet it goes really fast. Does it?"

"It does."

"Maybe you'll take me for a ride sometime?"

"Samuel."

"I'm leaving tomorrow."

"Oh."

"And even if he wasn't, Samuel, that's not something you ask our guests. We've talked about this, remember?" the boy's mother said while sliding her son a stern glare.

"Yes, ma'am."

Samuel glanced at Dominic and rolled his eyes, and yet again Dom found himself stifling a chuckle. And wondering at the last time he'd laughed so much in such a short span of time. "Tough break, kid."

"Let's get you checked in. Name?"

"Dominic Dunn."

"Domin—"

His name ended with a gasp and Ireland's eyes filled with tears. She blinked rapidly and managed to keep them from falling, but in that instant, he knew she recognized him—and knew his reason for being there.

CLICK THE LAST GOODBYE TO KEEP READING!

Also by Kay Lyons

MONTANA SECRETS SERIES:

- HEALING HER COWBOY
- IT HAD TO BE YOU
- HERS TO KEEP
- MILLION DOLLAR STANDOFF
- HIS CHRISTMAS WISH
- THEIR SECRET SON

THE SEASIDE SISTERS SERIES:

- THE LAST GOODBYE
- LATTES AND LULLABYES
- MAP OF DREAMS
- WORTH THE RISK
- LOST LOVE FOUND

TAMING THE TULANES SERIES:

- SMALL TOWN SCANDAL
- THEIR SECRET BARGAIN
- CROSSING THE LINE
- THE NANNY'S SECRET
- SOMEONE TO TRUST

THE STONE RIVER SERIES:

- WORTH THE WAIT

- NOT BY SIGHT
- THROUGH THE VALLEY
- LEAD ME NOT
- CHRISTMAS AT HOLLY WOOD
- THEIR CHRISTMAS MIRACLE
- SECOND CHANCES

SMALL TOWN SCANDALS SERIES:

- BRODY'S REDEMPTION
- FALLING FOR HER BOSS
- WITH THIS MAN

SECRET SANTA SERIES:

- SECRET SANTA
- SECRET SANTA II: A CHRISTMAS TO REMEMBER

MAKE ME A MATCH SERIES:

- ROMANCE RESET
- RULES OF ENGAGEMENT
- THE MATCHMAKER'S SECRET
- PERFECTLY MISMATCHED
- BY THE BOOK

About the Author

Kay Lyons always wanted to be a writer, ever since the age of seven or eight when she copied the pictures out of a Charlie Brown book and rewrote the story because she didn't like the plot. Through the years her stories have changed but one characteristic stayed true— they were all romances. Each and every one of her manuscripts included a love story.

Published in 2005 with Harlequin Enterprises, Kay's first release was a national bestseller. Kay has also been a HOLT Medallion, Book Buyers Best and RITA Award nominee. Look for her most recent novels with Kindred Spirits Publishing.

For more information regarding her work, please visit Kay at the following:

www.kaylyonsauthor.com

@KayLyonsAuthor (Twitter)

Kay Lyons Author (Facebook)

Author_Kay_Lyons (Instagram)

Kay Lyons, Author (Pinterest)

SIGN UP FOR KAY'S NEWSLETTER AND RECEIVE UPDATES ON NEW RELEASES, CONTESTS, PRE-RELEASE BOOK INFORMATION, EXCLUSIVES AND MORE!

FAQ

FAQ ABOUT THE MAKE ME A MATCH SERIES:

Is Carolina Cove a real place?

Carolina Cove is purely fictional; however, it is *loosely* based on one of my favorite places—Kure Beach, North Carolina. Kure Beach is home to a wonderful pier, a pavilion for special events like weddings and birthdays, swings facing the Atlantic, pelicans Pete and George, coffee shops, restaurants, and more. It's also close to the North Carolina Aquarium, Carolina Beach, and Wilmington.

Can I stay at the Carolina Cove Inn?

While Carolina Cove and the Carolina Cove Inn are purely fictional, there are plenty of motels and rentals in the area to enjoy.

But the pier is real?

Yes! And it has quite a history. Be sure to check out

the Kure Beach Pier Cam for a view of Kure Beach and the Atlantic.

What about the restaurants and coffee shops and places you've mentioned in the series?

London's Lattes is based on two of my favorite local coffee shops in Kure Beach and Carolina Beach. Are there more? Yes, plenty. But those two shops I know well because I've visited fairly often while writing these stories. Neither of them on their own was perfect for what I had in mind for London's, however, so I basically combined the two and ta-da! London's Lattes was born. But, no, if you go into either of them, you won't find London's exact business. Isn't fiction wonderful?

Why make up a city? Why not use Kure Beach?

One of the best things about writing fiction is that when a story appears a certain way, you can write it just that way. Carolina Cove and the characters appeared to me in story form and while Kure Beach IS one of my favorite places, I had to change some things to better fit the series as well as steer far away from any real-life persons/families for obvious reasons. Doing so, that meant also changing the name of the city, etc. But, that said, you will find a slew of similarities in the fictional city and the real one. :)

Where is the dream catcher mailbox?

Unfortunately the dream catcher mailbox is pure fiction and an idea taken from a "beach mailbox" I visited once many years ago. The dream catcher mailbox first appeared in the SEASIDE SISTERS SERIES.

How did you research the matchmaking aspect?

Oh, the answer to this was fun! Wilmington actually has a professional matchmaker. I interviewed her to get my details straight and learned a lot about a very fascinating business!

MAKE ME A MATCH SERIES:

- ROMANCE RESET
- RULES OF ENGAGEMENT
- THE MATCHMAKER'S SECRET
- PERFECTLY MISMATCHED
- BY THE BOOK